Janet slid her arm over Clint's chest. She was lying on her belly next to him while he was lying on his back. He put his hand on her back and was about to move it down when suddenly the door was kicked open and the room was filled with men with guns.

Because Janet was lying with her arm over him, his initial move for his gun was impeded just enough for them to get the drop on him.

"Don't," Jenkins said, pointing a shotgun at him. There were four other men with him. They all pointed guns at Clint.

"You sure you got enough men for this, Jenkins?" Clint asked. . . .

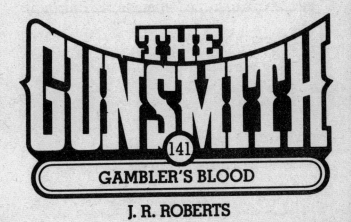

THE GUNSMITH

141

GAMBLER'S BLOOD

J. R. ROBERTS

JOVE BOOKS, NEW YORK

GAMBLER'S BLOOD

A Jove Book / published by arrangement with
the author

PRINTING HISTORY
Jove edition / September 1993

ISBN: 0-515-11196-1

Jove Books are published by The Berkley Publishing Group,
200 Madison Avenue, New York, New York 10016.
The name "JOVE" and the "J" logo
are trademarks belonging to Jove Publications, Inc.

PRINTED IN THE UNITED STATES OF AMERICA

10 9 8 7 6 5 4 3 2 1

THE GUNSMITH

141

GAMBLER'S BLOOD

ONE

Clint Adams had never been to Gambler's Fork before. Oh, he'd been invited, but it always seemed that there was somewhere else he had to be or something else he had to do. This time, however, the game fell right in the middle of a big nothing-to-do.

"Gambler's Fork," Rick Hartman said.

He was sitting across from Clint in his saloon, Rick's Place, which was located in Labyrinth, Texas. Clint was holding in his hand the telegram that was his invitation to the Gambler's Fork game.

"That's that big Arkansas game, right?" Hartman asked. "Some rich rancher who likes to rub shoulders with the good, the bad, and the ugly?"

Clint raised his eyebrows at Hartman and said, "That's very poetic, Rick."

Hartman smiled and said proudly, "And I just made it up, too."

1

"I didn't know you had it in you."

"Hey," Hartman said, with a big smile, "I'm a surprising kind of guy."

"Well, the rancher's name is Bartock, Harry Bartock," Clint explained, "and he's been having this game for the past five years or so."

"Wait a minute," Hartman said, frowning, trying to dredge something up from the recesses of his memory. He snapped his fingers and asked, "Weren't you invited to this thing last year?"

Clint nodded and said, "And the year before. Couldn't go either time."

"Know anybody who *has* gone?"

Clint nodded again.

"Bat went."

Hartman wrinkled his nose and said, "Masterson." Rick Hartman and Bat Masterson did not get along at all. "Anyone else?"

"I think Luke Short went one year."

"So much for the good guys," Hartman said. "What about the bad guys?"

"Well," Clint said, "if you can believe the stories, all sorts of bad men have played in that game. Vince Taylor, for one."

It was Hartman's turn to raise his eyebrows.

"Hey, last year's baddest bad guy," he said.

"They come and go, don't they?" Clint said.

"We all do, don't we?" Hartman said. "So, you gonna go and play?"

"Well," Clint said, folding the telegram neatly, "I've got nothing better to do this year."

"Then I guess that takes care of the ugly," Hartman said with a big grin, "don't it?"

"You keep getting more and more clever, don't you?" Clint asked.

"Well—"

"In your old age," Clint said as he stood up.

"Hey!"

"I've got to send a reply to this," Clint said. "Think up some more clever things to say while I'm gone."

Harry Bartock looked up as his man, Jenkins, entered his office. He didn't call Jenkins a butler, even though they would have done so in some of the more genteel parts of the country and the world. No, he preferred to refer to Jenkins simply as his "man."

Jenkins was in his mid-forties, a solidly built man who performed a wide variety of tasks for Bartock and seemed to have absolutely no limitations whatsoever. He had bushy black eyebrows which stood out in stark contrast to his gleaming bald head. He had a first name, but he didn't like it, and Bartock never used it. Few men did and enjoyed their teeth for very much longer than the time it took to say it.

"Yes, Jenkins?"

"Another acceptance telegram, sir."

"Oh, good," Bartock said, rubbing his hands together. "Who is it this time?"

"Clint Adams, sir."

Bartock's eyes widened as he said gleefully, "The Gunsmith?"

"Yes, sir."

"Well," Bartock said, rubbing his hands together, "finally. We've been inviting him for a couple of years, haven't we, Jenkins?"

"Yes, sir."

"And he's finally coming," Bartock said. "How many does that make, Jenkins?"

"Six, sir."

"And with me, that's seven," Bartock said. "Jenkins, we have a game, don't we?"

"Yes, sir," Jenkins said, "we do."

Among other jobs Jenkins performed, he was the house dealer for the game.

"All right, Jenkins," Bartock said, "thank you. You can have the rest of the night off."

Jenkins nodded and withdrew.

Bartock put down his pencil and closed the ledger book he was working on. People who did business with him were often surprised when they met him. No one expected the successful rancher and businessman Harry Bartock to be twenty-nine years old—and he knew he looked even younger. He always enjoyed the look of surprise in their eyes.

He picked up his pencil and wrote down the names of the six players who had accepted his invitation this year. It was quite a list. Usually, he'd get at least three players who were wanted somewhere for something. This time there were four, and one questionable—and the Gunsmith.

The Gunsmith . . .

Bartock's ranch, during the game, was neutral ground. He'd actually had lawmen and bad men sit at the same table and put aside that fact during the game. Once, there was a bounty hunter who was hunting the man who was sitting across the table from him, and they *still* played each other. Bartock heard that the bounty hunter killed the bad man about an hour after they left the ranch, but that was not his concern. His only rule was that there was to be none of that in his home—and he had Jenkins and some of *his* men around to enforce that rule.

TWO

When Clint Adams rode into Gambler's Fork, Arkansas, he was looking forward to nothing more than some well-played, competitive poker. Of course, he was also looking forward to winning some money, but for him the enjoyment was mostly in the playing. He knew he wasn't going to win or lose enough money to change his life.

He rode Duke, his big, black gelding, over to the livery stable. He told the man there he wasn't sure how long he would be staying. While the invitation was for poker, he wasn't sure whether he'd be staying in a hotel in town or at Bartock's ranch. The invitation was not specific on that point.

Carrying his saddlebags and rifle he walked to the hotel and took a room. He told the clerk the same story. He wasn't sure when he'd be leaving.

"Are you here for the game, mister?" the clerk asked.

"What game?" Clint asked.

The clerk looked at his name on the register and then looked at Clint's face closely. Clint could see by the look on the man's face that he knew the name. What Clint didn't know was whether the man had been put on the lookout for him or if he was just recognizing the name from his reputation.

"You're here for Mr. Bartock's game," the clerk said. "Everybody in town knows about the game, mister. It's no secret."

"So?"

"So Mr. Bartock usually gives his players the choice of staying at the ranch or staying in town."

"And what do people usually decide?"

"Let's put it this way," the clerk said. "I wouldn't take more than one day's payment in advance from you."

"Okay," Clint said, "if you know so much, are there any other players in town yet?"

"No," the clerk said, shaking his head. "You're the first one—and *you're* a day early."

"I made better time than I anticipated," Clint said. "Anything in town to do to pass the time?"

"Oh, sure," the clerk said. "We got two saloons, and you can find some action at either one."

"The town lives up to its name, huh?"

"These days it does," the clerk said. "In the old days I think it was just a name. You know, like any other name? It didn't really mean nothin'."

"Not like that now, huh?"

"Oh no," the man said. "Now we live up to the name."

There was a moment of silence, and then Clint said, "Can I have my key, please?"

"Oh, sure, Mr. Adams, sure," the clerk said. "Here you go. Number four, upstairs."

"Thank you." Clint picked up his saddlebags and rifle and then asked the man, "Is there another hotel in town?"

"One more," the clerk said, "but believe me, none of the other players is in town yet."

"You keep track, huh?"

"Well," the clerk said, "it is a pretty big game, ain't it?"

"I don't know," Clint said. "Is it?"

"You'll find out when you get there, won't you?"

"I guess I will," Clint said, then went upstairs to his room.

The room was nothing special, much like a lot of other rooms he'd been in. He looked out the window at the main street, which was also just like any other town. So far, Gambler's Fork was nothing special, but he expected that would change, especially if the town lived up to its name.

He decided to go out right then and there and give it a fair chance to do just that.

Downstairs he walked over to the desk again.

"Room all right?" the clerk asked.

"It's fine."

"Help you with somethin'?"

"What time do things usually get started in town?" Clint asked.

"Well, it's already three," the clerk said.

"Things should be in full swing just about now."

"Tell me something," Clint said, "what kind of law do you have in this town?"

"Understanding," the man said, "real understanding."

THREE

Clint had his choice of two saloons in town, and he simply picked the first one he came to. It was called the Fourth Ace Saloon. He walked inside and saw that what the hotel clerk had said was true. There were half a dozen gaming tables around the room, and they all had people two rows deep. The place was indeed in full swing.

He walked to the bar, which was not as crowded as the tables, found a spot, and ordered a cold beer.

"Just get into town?" the bartender asked.

"That's right," Clint said, lifting the beer and taking a gulp.

"Here for the game?"

Clint frowned. He'd been to private games before, but the operative word in those cases had always been "private." In this case it seemed like everyone in town knew about the game.

"What game is that?" he asked.

"Private game," the bartender said, "out at the

10

Bartock ranch. Guess you ain't here for it if you don't know about it."

"Guess not," Clint said, playing it cool.

"Well, there's plenty of action right here," the bartender said.

"Sure looks like it."

Clint turned with his beer in his hand to take a look at the room. He saw blackjack, faro, roulette, and poker going on. There were two poker tables, both with house dealers, and two black-jack tables. The dealers were all men. There were four women working the room. They all looked to be between twenty and thirty, and they were all pretty. There wasn't one of the four who looked used up. He was sure that the place was owned by someone who made an effort to keep fresh girls on the premises. A man will buy a drink from a pretty girl even if he's not thirsty.

"What's your pleasure?"

He had seen the girl approaching him. She was dark-haired and pretty, probably about twenty-four. Her mouth was wide, and her smile made it even wider.

"Poker," he said, "but not usually against the house."

"They don't allow private games in here," she said, frowning.

"I didn't think they would."

"Of course," she added, "if you're looking for a private game—"

"Not really," he said, glancing at her and then looking around the room.

"Well . . . what about something other than poker?"

"No thanks."

"What about something . . . other than gambling?" she asked.

He looked directly at her this time and asked, "What are you offering me?"

"Just what you see," she said, putting her hands on her hips. She was about five feet four, built solidly but not lushly.

"For a price," he said, "of course."

"Well, of course," she said.

He shook his head and said, "No thanks."

She regarded him for a moment, then said, "Don't like to pay for it, huh?"

"That's right."

"Well," she said, taking her hands off her hips and turning, "a girl's got to make a living."

"Everybody has to make a living."

"My name's Wendy," she said, "if you decide to change your mind."

"I won't, Wendy, but thanks anyway."

"Sure, mister . . ."

He watched her walk away to find a more likely candidate to pay for her charms.

To pass the time he decided to drop a few chips on a number in roulette. He didn't like blackjack. The largest return you got on your money was two and a half to one, and that was if you made blackjack. Faro wasn't his game either. If he wanted to pass the time that left poker and roulette, and he had been telling the truth about not liking to play poker against the house. You were playing against a built-in advantage. Of course, the same was true of roulette, but he had no

strategy in mind. He was simply going to buy
some chips and play a number. If it came out, it
came out, if it didn't . . . all he'd lose was a few
bucks and some time.

He walked over to a clerk behind a cage and
bought some five-dollar chips, a hundred dollars'
worth. It did not come out of the money he had
brought for the poker game. And if he happened
to win, this money would not go *into* the poker
game.

"Good luck," the clerk said.

"Thanks," he said, "I'll need it."

The clerk was an old man whose mouth had
collapsed into itself. If he had any teeth left it
was only one or two.

"Just play your lucky number, sonny," he said.
"That always works."

"Thanks, Pop," Clint said. "The only problem
is, I don't have one."

The old man cackled and said, "That ain't no
problem, sonny. You can use mine."

"And what's yours?"

The man cackled again and said, "Thirty-six."

"And why is that?"

" 'Cause double it and that's how old I am."

Clint shrugged and said, "That sounds like as
good a reason as any, Pop. Thanks."

FOUR

He played number thirty-six twenty times with a five-dollar chip and never came close. In fact, he didn't think that a number with a three had come up at all. No thirties, no thirteen, not even the number three. That's the way it went sometimes.

He went back to the bar and ordered another beer.

"No luck?" the bartender asked.

"Not a nibble."

"Hey," the man said, "try again, you never know when your luck will change."

"Maybe not," Clint said, "but you have to know when not to push it."

"Nah," the bartender said, "my theory is push it till it breaks."

"Fine," Clint said, "that's the way you think."

"Hey, mister," the bartender said, "if you want to make money—"

"Hey," Clint said, cutting the man off sharply, "is it your job to pour beer or shill for the house?"

The man looked stunned for a moment and then said, "Hey, I was just tryin' to help—"

"Yeah," Clint said, "but who? Look, you want to give advice, find some beginner to give it to, all right?"

"Sure, mister, sure," the bartender said. "No offense. Hey, if you know what you're doin' that's fine. I'll go and . . . and pour some beer."

Clint watched as the man sidled down the bar, throwing a cautious glance his way once or twice. He didn't know why he'd gotten so angry. Maybe because he didn't like being hustled. He was sure that the bartender's line had probably sent men right back to the tables before. Maybe it *was* the man's job to pour beer *and* shill for the house. He just didn't want the man thinking he was somebody who could be hustled.

He decided to finish the beer he was working on and then go take a look at the other saloon. After that he'd be ready to eat supper.

It was after six p.m. when Cort Mason rode into Gambler's Fork. He was the second of the invited players to arrive. He registered at the other hotel in town, and then went over to the Fourth Ace Saloon. By that time Clint Adams had left the Ace and was across the street at the Double Zero Saloon.

Cort Mason was a gambler and a good one. That was how he made his living. At thirty-eight, he'd been plying his trade for exactly half his life. In the "good" man/"bad" man scheme of things, he was the one who would have had to be considered on the borderline. He had played in Bartock's game once, the first year he'd held it, and he had done quite well for himself. Now, five years later, he felt it was time to go back to that well once again.

The next players to arrive rode in together. They knew each other, and while they did not habitually ride as a pair, they figured since they were both heading the same way this time they might as well ride together.

Tim Easter and Jim Griffith spent most of their time on the wrong side of the law. Easter, thirty-three, felt that he was entitled to anything he could lay his hands on, no matter who had it before he did. Griffith, thirty-five, enjoyed holding up stagecoaches. He liked the variety of people you were able to hold up that way. In addition to their reputations in their chosen professions, the two were both known as good poker players.

They left their horses at the livery and went to register at the same hotel Cort Mason was in.

"Look," Easter said, pointing to Mason's name in the register.

"Cort Mason," Griffith said. "You know him?"

"Only by reputation," Easter said. "He's supposed to be one helluva poker player."

"Well," Griffith said, "this game might be interestin' after all."

They registered, each taking his own room. Both men decided to freshen up and then go looking for something to eat.

"Should we look Mason up?" Easter asked.

"I don't see why we should," Griffith said.

"Why not?"

"Well, we know he's here, and probably for the big game, right?"

"Right."

"So that gives us an advantage," Griffith said. "Even if he sees our names in the register, chances are he won't know us from Adam."

"I don't know," Easter said, "I like to think I have a little reputation."

"Little is right," Griffith said. "Compared to Mason's rep, Tim, we're tinhorns."

"Hey!"

"Of course," Griffith added, "by the time we're done here, all of that might be changed, huh?"

"Right," Easter said with a nod.

"So then why give up our advantage?" Griffith said. "He'll meet us when he meets everyone else, at the table. Right?"

"Right," Easter said.

"I'm gonna take a bath," Griffith said, "and then we can get somethin' to eat."

"A bath?"

"Yeah," Griffith said. "A bath and maybe a shave. That's what *I* meant by freshenin' up. What did you have in mind?"

"I don't know," Easter said, frowning. "I can't rightly say I've ever freshened up before."

"You ever take a bath before?" Griffith asked.

"Sure," Easter said, then added, "a few times."

"Well, take my advice," Griffith said, "make it at least one more time. . . ."

• • •

The two remaining players would not arrive a
day early in Gambler's Fork as the first four had.
They would arrive precisely on time for the first
meeting at Harry Bartock's house, which was to
take place the next evening, at dinner. Tradition-
ally, that was when all of the players met each
other and their host.

FIVE

Clint left the Double Zero armed with directions to a decent place to eat dinner. The bartender in the Zero was less talkative than the one in the Ace, but more helpful. Part of the reason for that was, as crowded as the Ace had been, the Zero was clearly the more popular of the two saloons. They did not need the bartender to also act as a shill. It was larger, brighter, more crowded, and had more gaming tables than its competition across the street. Also, as well as having beautiful girls working the floor, they had two lovely female blackjack dealers.

Clint had known a lot of casino owners, and the thinking behind attractive dealers was sound. Men almost always want to impress a pretty girl, and in doing so they will sometimes play foolishly—more foolishly than if a man were dealing.

Two of the girls in the Zero had approached Clint and tried to entice him with their charms. Either would have done fine, except that they expected to be paid. This was a hard-and-fast rule that Clint adhered to. He did quite well with women, and he saw no need to pay for one. Regretfully, he told both women that he was not interested in paying for their wares.

After two beers he had asked the bartender where he could get something to eat.

"What are you interested in?" the man asked.

"A decent steak."

The man gave him directions to Red's, a small restaurant where he could not only get a decent steak, but an excellent one.

Clint thanked the man, paid for the beers, and left.

As Clint Adams was leaving the Double Zero, both Tim Easter and Jim Griffith were leaving the Fourth Ace.

"Hey," Griffith said, putting his hand against Easter's chest to stop him, "isn't that . . . yeah, that is him, ain't it?"

"Who?" Easter asked, looking around. "It's who?"

"Across the street there, walking away from the other saloon. That's Clint Adams!"

"Adams?" Easter said, squinting in an attempt to spot the man in question. "Ain't he . . . the Gunsmith?"

"He sure is," Griffith said. "That's him, ain't it? Over there?"

Finally, Easter spotted the man and took a look.

"I dunno," he said. "I ain't never seen the Gunsmith before."

"Well, I have," Griffith said, "twice, and both

times I was damned glad he wasn't after me. I saw him outdraw three men . . . cold! None of them ever got their guns out."

"Aw," Easter said, giving his friend a look, "that ain't possible."

Griffith looked at Easter and said solemnly, "I'm tellin' you, none of them men ever cleared leather. It was . . . amazin'!"

Easter looked down the street at the retreating back of Clint Adams.

"What's he doin' here?" he wondered aloud.

"What the heck do you think he's doin' here?" Griffith asked. "He's here for the game."

"Him, too?" Easter asked. "This is gonna be some game, huh?"

"With Adams *and* Mason . . . and *us*?" Griffith asked. "It sure is."

"I wonder who else is gonna show up?" Easter asked.

"I dunno," Griffith said, "but it sure is gonna be interestin' to find out. Come on, let's go check that other saloon."

Cort Mason was coming out of the hotel when he spotted the man walking toward him. He stepped back quickly into the hotel lobby and then moved over to the front window. Through it he watched as the man passed close enough for him to positively identify him.

Clint Adams!

So, the Gunsmith was in town. And for what other reason than to play in Harry Bartock's game?

Mason had been wondering all the way here whom he'd end up playing against in this game. There were a handful of players he looked forward to playing again and again, and an even smaller group he looked forward to playing against for the very first time.

Clint Adams—the Gunsmith—was on that second list.

Mason had never played against Adams, but he'd heard stories about the man being as good with a deck of cards as he was with a gun. Of course, given Adams's reputation with a gun, that was hard to believe, but Cort Mason looked forward to finding out firsthand whether it was true or not.

Naturally, being the kind of man who welcomed quality competition, he hoped it *was* true. That would make it all the more sweet when he came out of the game the big winner.

SIX

The bartender at the Double Zero was right. The steak Clint had at Red's was excellent, cooked just exactly the way he liked it. That was because Red, who owned the place and did all the cooking, had asked him when he ordered the steak exactly how he liked it.

"You tell me what color you want it to be on the outside," Red had said, "and what color you want it to be on the inside when you cut it open, how much you want it to bleed. Just tell me *exactly* how you want your steak, mister, and that's how I'll cook it for you."

"Adams," he said.

"What?"

"My name is Clint Adams," he said, "but if you cook my steak exactly the way I like it, you can call me Clint."

Red stood up straight, put her hands on her hips, and stared down at him.

"And you can call me Red."

"Okay."

Red was a surprise. He watched her walk back to the kitchen and then thought about her when she was out of sight.

For one thing there wasn't anything "red" about her. She was blond, looked to be in her late thirties. She had clear, pale skin, hazel eyes, and a vitality that he noticed as soon as she approached his table. She had the vitality of youth, and he wondered how she had managed to hold onto that. He wished she could teach him the trick.

And she could cook.

"Well?" she asked after he'd cut into the steak the first time.

He put the piece in his mouth, chewed slowly, and swallowed before answering.

"It's perfect," he said, with a smile. "I can't believe it, but I think it's the first perfect steak I've ever had in my life."

"Well, not the last," she promised, "not if you eat here again. From now on when you come in, I'll make it exactly that way."

He put another piece in his mouth and said, "I like steak with my eggs, for breakfast."

"You come back tomorrow morning," she said, "and that's what you'll get."

He watched her with her other customers. She talked to them all, and when they finished eating, they all left satisfied.

He ate slowly, so that eventually he was the last person in the place.

"More coffee?" she asked.

"Of course," he said, "even your coffee is perfect."

"Well," she said, "if you promise not to tell anyone, I'll tell you my secret."

"Really?"

"Yes," she said, nodding. "Let me get you that coffee, and then I'll tell you."

She went into the kitchen and came out with another pot of coffee and a fresh cup.

"Do you mind if I have one with you?" she asked.

"No, of course not," he said. "Please."

She sat down opposite him, filled his cup and then her own.

"Okay," he said. "What's the secret?"

"Well," she said, sitting back in her chair, "the secret to why I can cook perfectly is . . . I'm a goddess."

He hesitated, then said, "A what?"

"A goddess," she said. "You know what a goddess is, don't you?"

"Well . . . sure . . ."

"Like the gods and goddesses on Mount Olympus?" she said. "The Greek gods?"

"Well," he said, "I don't know about Greek goddesses, but I have heard of some Indian gods and goddesses."

"Same thing," she said. "You see, you have to have divine powers in order to do anything perfectly."

"That . . . makes sense," Clint said, slowly. He still couldn't tell whether or not she was serious.

"Of course it does," she said, "so I have divine powers over food . . . and drink," she added, raising her coffee cup.

There was an awkward moment of silence, and then Clint said, "Well, whatever the reason is, I'm glad I got a chance to sample your cooking, Miss—"

"Red," she said, "just Red."

"Red," he said.

He finished his cup of coffee and then paid her for the meal.

"You come back in the morning," she said, walking him to the door, "and I'll be ready for you.

"Okay," he said, "I'll be back. I doubt I'll eat anywhere else in town while I'm here."

"How long will you be here?" she asked.

"In town?" he asked. "I'm not sure. I'll be in the area for a while, though."

"Oh," she said, "you're here for the game, aren't you?"

He frowned and hesitated, but she spoke again before he could answer.

"Never mind," she said, waving her hand in front of her face as if shooing flies away, "don't answer that. It's none of my business. Good night, Clint."

"Good night, Red."

As he stepped outside, she stood in the doorway, leaning against the door frame.

"You didn't believe all of that, did you?" she asked.

"All of what?"

"All that stuff about being a divine goddess."

He stared at her for a long moment and then said, "Well, of course I believed it."

She smiled at him then and said, "Good."

SEVEN

"What are you so quiet about?" Tim Easter asked Jim Griffith.

"Huh?"

They were sitting at a table in the Double Zero. It was getting late, and the place was less than half full. A couple of the gaming tables had closed and were covered with cloth.

"You been real quiet for a while," Easter said. "What are you thinkin' about?"

For a moment he thought Griffith *still* didn't hear him, but then the other man looked right at him.

"I'm thinkin' about makin' a killin'," Griffith said.

"Well, sure," Easter said, "that's what we came here to do, isn't it?"

"No," Griffith said, "I ain't talkin' about cards, Timmy."

"No?" Easter said, with a puzzled frown. "Then what *are* you talkin' about?"

"Somethin' else," Griffith said. "I'm talkin' about somethin' *big*."

Easter waited a few moments and when Griffith didn't say anything else he said, "Well, are you gonna let me in on it or what?"

"Sure," Griffith said, after a minute, "sure, Tim, I'm gonna let you in on it. . . ."

Cort Mason had kept a low profile since arriving in Gambler's Fork. It wasn't hard to do. He wasn't interested in seeing any more of the town than he had seen when he rode in. After all, he hadn't come there to see the town. He also wasn't interested in their saloons, because he hadn't come to play poker in a saloon game.

The only time he left his room after seeing Clint Adams was to get dinner in the hotel dining room. He had also taken an opportunity to check the desk register, so he knew that Adams wasn't staying in his hotel. Even if he was, though, Clint Adams would not recognize *him* on sight the way he had Adams. Still, he didn't like seeing an opponent before the actual game. He knew that they were all to meet and have dinner at Bartock's ranch the next night; what he didn't know was whether or not the game would start that same night, after dinner. He hoped it would. He didn't want to waste any time.

After dinner he went back to his room and played some solitaire while sitting on the bed. He wondered briefly if he should bother getting himself a girl. After all, once they started playing he wouldn't even think about women until the game was over—even if it went on for days. He considered asking the desk clerk to get him one, then decided against it. It was getting late, and he was tired from his ride. Besides, after he finished with the girl, she might expect him to talk to her. He didn't feel up to that. He was thirty-eight years old and had never quite gotten the knack of talking to a woman.

He threw the deck of cards he'd been playing solitaire with away. He couldn't abide a deck of cards once it had already been used. He would demand a new deck every hour he was in a game, and no one ever minded. Everybody liked fresh cards. His favorite smell in the world was the smell of a fresh deck of cards.

He imagined that he could smell it even as he drifted off to sleep.

Clint Adams went back to the Fourth Ace for another beer before turning in. He did not consciously pick that saloon over the other. It was simply the one he passed on his way to the hotel.

The place had quieted down quite a bit, and all but one table had been covered with cloth for the night. The girls were gone. They had either turned in or found men who were willing to pay for their company.

He ordered a beer, and the bartender, who remembered him very well, served it and then walked to the other end of the bar. He kept casting hurt looks Clint's way.

Clint thought briefly about Red and her claims to be a goddess. He had decided that she was kidding . . . sort of. He liked her, though. He decided that he would certainly go back there for breakfast tomorrow and probably lunch. If it wasn't for the poker game, he might have tried to get to know her better.

He shook his head and finished his beer. In this kind of game, it wouldn't pay to have anything else on your mind but cards.

"Hey!" he called to the bartender.

"Huh? Me?" the man said, surprised that Clint had spoken to him.

"Yeah, you," Clint said. "Thanks for the beer."

"Oh, uh, sure," the man stammered. "Anytime."

Clint left the saloon and went back to his hotel to turn in.

EIGHT

When Harry Bartock awoke the next morning he was excited. That was the way he always felt the morning that his guests were going to arrive.

In truth, this year he'd had to settle for some guests who were a bit lower on his list than in the past. Still, he felt that the presence of a poker player like Cort Mason, and of course the Gunsmith himself, would—*should*—make up for that.

At breakfast he said to Jenkins, "Are the ladies arranged for, Jenkins?"

"They are, sir," Jenkins said. "They will be here at least two hours before the guests are scheduled to arrive tonight."

"Good," Bartock said. He leaned over and sniffed at the bowl of scrambled eggs before he put some onto his plate. He took some bacon next. "Is the room set up?"

"Yes, sir," Jenkins said. "The other furniture has been moved out, and the table is in the center of the room. I have set up a small bar."

"Excellent. Do we have enough cards?" Bartock spooned some marmalade onto his toast. "You know Mr. Mason's proclivity for fresh decks."

"I know it quite well, sir," Jenkins said. "I have taken care of that."

"And the guest rooms?" Bartock asked. "They're all set up?"

"They are, sir," the other man said. "Fresh linen and towels, and a bathtub in each room. I have hired extra help to fetch water in the morning. None of your guests will have to wait if they want a bath."

"I can always count on you, can't I, Jenkins?" Bartock said.

"I believe you can, sir," Jenkins said. "Enjoy your breakfast."

"Thank you, Jenkins," Bartock said.

He sat at his huge dining room table, eating his breakfast alone. He wondered idly what the always proper Jenkins would say if he ever invited the man to sit and eat with him? Probably shock the poor fellow. Hell, if he did that he'd shock himself! The only time Harry Bartock ever ate with anyone was during the days when his poker game was going on. Under normal circumstances, Bartock preferred his own company to all others', and the more room he had the better. Even when he enjoyed the company of a woman in his bed, she had to leave when they were finished. He couldn't abide sleeping in the same bed with a woman.

Harry Bartock knew that some people saw him as eccentric, but he didn't care. He was wealthy enough to live the way he wanted to live, and that's what was important to him.

Mentally, he went over his guest list. Again he was pleased with all of his guests save two—the men named Easter and Griffith—and they were invited simply to fill out the table. Also, their reputations would add a little spice to the proceedings—although, admittedly, Jenkins had to *tell* him that the men had reputations. He himself had never heard of them.

Then, of course, there were Cort Mason and Clint Adams. *That* would be an interesting confrontation.

There was also something else interesting about this game. A player had been recommended to him, someone named Paul Harrison. He had never heard of the man, but his information was that he was an excellent poker player. Bartock always looked forward to discovering new blood.

And then there was the sixth and final player. He was sure that *this* player's appearance would be a total surprise to all of the others.

Sitting there alone at his huge dining room table, Harry Bartock smiled. He looked forward to seeing the expressions on their faces when he introduced that sixth player.

NINE

Clint had breakfast at Red's and was greeted warmly by the self-professed goddess.

"Steak and eggs?" she asked as he seated himself.

"What else?"

"I'll bring the coffee out first," she said.

He had risen early, so only a few of her tables were occupied. There were two tables taken by what appeared to be married couples—one in their fifties and comfortable with each other, and one in their twenties and still starry-eyed—and another occupied by two men who were probably merchants, having their breakfast before opening up for the day's business.

She returned with the coffee and poured it out for him and then said, "The steak and eggs will be up in a couple of minutes."

"Take your time," he said. "I'm not in a hurry."

"Nowhere to go and nothing to do?" she asked.

"Not until this evening."

"Then you have time for a nice leisurely breakfast," she said. "I'll bring out a basket of biscuits and some butter."

"Sounds good."

Clint had taken a table that was up against a wall and was sitting so that he could see the door. He noticed when two men entered, looked around, and seemed to take some time to pick out a table, even though there were plenty available. In the end, they chose the table that was the farthest from him. He frowned, because he knew by their attempts *not* to look at him that they had recognized him.

Red came out of the kitchen, put the basket of biscuits and the butter on the table, and then went over to take the orders of the two men who had just entered. Clint couldn't hear what they were saying, but one man appeared to be very interested in either her menu or her. It took them a while to place their order, and when Red turned to walk back to the kitchen, Clint could see the look of frustration on her pretty face.

Clint studied the two men while buttering a flaky, warm biscuit. He didn't recognize either man, but he knew the type. They traveled, they made their living whatever way they could, whether inside the law or out. They gambled, not only with cards but with lives—their own and others'. And judging from Red's reaction to talking to them, they had no manners around a woman.

He slipped a piece of biscuit into his mouth and marveled at how it melted there. He was eating his second when Red came back out of the kitchen carrying a coffeepot and cups to the two men's table.

"What about some of those biscuits?" Jim Griffith asked her.

She turned and looked at Clint, who was enjoying the biscuits.

"I have to make another batch," she said to Griffith. "If they're ready while you're still here, I'll bring some out."

"You do that," Griffith said, taking hold of her wrist after she had finished pouring the coffee. "You bring 'em out as soon as they're done, huh, honey?"

"Let go of my arm, please," she said.

"What's the matter?" he asked, grinning. "You don't like when a man touches you?"

"I like to pick the man, if you don't mind."

She was holding the pot of coffee in her right hand, and that was the wrist he had grabbed.

"If you don't let go," she warned, "I'll pour the rest of this hot coffee in your lap."

Griffith's eyes caught hers and he asked, "Do you have the nerve to do that?"

"Try me," she said, without a smile.

"I think she does, Jim," Tim Easter said. "I truly think that she does."

Griffith studied her face for a few more moments and then released her arm and said, "Yeah, Tim, I believe you're right."

She set the coffeepot down on the table with a bang and said, "Your breakfast will be ready shortly."

As she stalked away, Tim Easter laughed and said, "I don't think she likes you, Jim."

Griffith fixed Easter with a hard stare and said, "She just has to get to know me, is all. Don't worry, she'll like me."

The woman called Red—whose full name was Janet Munro—went back into the kitchen and rubbed her wrist where the man had held it. She wouldn't let *him* know that he had hurt her. She was glad that he had looked into her eyes and saw that she *would* indeed have dumped the hot coffee into his lap. She did not like being pawed, especially not by animals like those two. She hoped that they would eat their breakfast, pay their bill—*especially* pay their bill—and leave without further incident.

Somehow, though, she knew that—like with a lot of things in her life—she was hoping in vain.

TEN

"He saw us come in," Easter said nervously.

"Of course he saw us come in, Tim," Griffith said. "That's how he's stayed alive this long, by noticing people."

"Well then, he's seen us."

"So what?" Griffith said. "He doesn't know who we are. We have just as much right to eat here as he does, don't we?"

"Well, yeah . . . I guess. . . ."

"Damned right we do," Griffith said. "Where's that gal with my flapjacks?"

At that moment Red came out of the kitchen carrying Clint's breakfast.

"Mmmm," Easter said, sniffing the air, "I smell steak and eggs."

"Steak and eggs!" Griffith said. "That's what I'm gonna order."

"You already ordered," Easter said.

"So what? I'll change my order."

"But the gal probably already started cooking the flapjacks," Easter reasoned.

"So what? Let her throw them out. I want steak and eggs now." Griffith raised his chin and called out across the room, "Hey, honey. Over here!"

Red had just finished setting Clint's breakfast on the table when she heard Griffith call out for her from across the room.

"Oh," she said, "I hate being called 'honey.' "

"Are they giving you some trouble, Red?" Clint asked.

She straightened up and said, "Oh, no, nothing I can't handle. Enjoy your breakfast."

She turned and walked across the room to the table where Easter and Griffith were seated.

"Can I help you?" she asked.

"Yeah," Griffith said, "I want steak and eggs."

"In addition to the flapjacks?" she asked.

"No, *instead* of the flapjacks," Griffith said, annoyed. "Why would I want flapjacks *and* steak and eggs?"

"I don't know, sir," she said. "Why would you order flapjacks, and then steak and eggs?"

"Because I changed my mind. Is that a problem?"

"Well, I already started cooking the flapjacks—" she started.

"So? I ain't payin' for flapjacks."

Red stared at him for a moment, then decided that it wasn't worth an argument.

"All right, sir," she said. "I'll bring you some steak and eggs." She looked at Easter and asked, "Would you like to change your order, too?"

"Uh, no, that's all right, ma'am," Easter said, "I'll just take the flapjacks that I ordered."

"Hey," Griffith said, "if you want steak and eggs, Tim, make her make you steak and eggs."

"It's okay, Jim," Easter said, obviously embarrassed, "I'll eat the flapjacks I ordered."

"Well, not me," Griffith said, "I want steak and eggs, like I ordered."

"Yes, sir," she said. "I'll bring it out."

"And what about those biscuits?"

"As soon as they're ready, sir."

"Well, hurry it up."

As she hurried away, Griffith laughed and said to Easter, "You got to show them who's boss, Tim. That's the way women like to be treated."

"I—I can't treat a woman like that, Jim," Tim Easter said. "It—it don't seem right."

"You puzzle me, Tim," Griffith said. "I seen you blow a man's head off for no good reason other than he stepped on your foot, and you can't talk to a woman the way one's supposed to be talked to?"

"It's different with a man," Easter said. "I just . . . ain't comfortable around womenfolk."

"Well, stick with me, then," Griffith said, "and I'll teach you how to make the womenfolk uncomfortable around *you*."

Tim Easter frowned. He didn't know if he wanted *that*, either, but he decided not to say what he was thinking.

"Sure, Jim," he said.

It just seemed easier than arguing.

Clint ate his breakfast with one eye on the two men. He was expecting trouble from them.

He had been expecting it from the moment they entered, but he hadn't been sure what form it would take. It seemed that one of them had his eye on Red, and maybe she wasn't responding to him the way he wanted, so he was giving her a hard time.

Clint hated men who gave women a hard time. His breakfast was delicious, but he was more concerned with what was going on across the room than he was with eating it.

He was going to hold *that* against the two men, as well.

ELEVEN

As it turned out, they were all able to finish their breakfast before the trouble started.

Red served Griffith his new order of steak and eggs and gave Easter his flapjacks. She was relieved when both men ate, and she actually had hopes of getting paid *and* getting rid of them.

Clint, who finished his breakfast well before the other two, had another pot of coffee and nursed it. He didn't want to leave until the other two men did.

"I know I said you could have a leisurely breakfast," Red said, teasing him, "but this is a little ridiculous, don't you think?"

"Do you need the table?"

"Oh no," she said, "I didn't mean that."

"Because I don't want to leave until they do," he said, jerking his chin across the room at the two men.

She turned and looked at them, and then looked back at him. Her face softened.

"That's so sweet of you, Clint," she said, "but

42

I think everything will be all right."

"Just the same," he said, "as long as you don't need the table . . ."

"You can stay as long as you like, Clint," she said, putting her hand on his shoulder.

She went off to collect money from some of her other customers and then went back into the kitchen. Across the room the two troublesome men appeared to be nearing the end of their meal.

"Hey, this was good," Easter said to Griffith. "You shoulda stuck with the flapjacks, Jim."

"Oh yeah?" Griffith said. Even though his steak and eggs had been delicious, he said, "Maybe the lady shoulda told me that."

"Well, she tried—"

"Maybe I won't pay for breakfast," Griffith said, pushing his plate away.

Easter frowned.

"You want me to pay for it?" he asked. "I don't know if I got enough—"

"No," Griffith said, "I mean *we* ain't payin'."

"We ain't?"

"No," Griffith said, "we ain't."

At that point Red came over and asked them, "Can I get you anything else?"

"I'm disappointed in you, sweetheart," Jim Griffith said.

She frowned.

"Why is that?"

"My friend says the flapjacks were real good."

"They always are," she said.

"Ha!" Griffith said. "Modest, ain't ya?"

"I don't have to be modest, mister," she said. "I'm the best cook in town."

"Yeah, well maybe you ought to take better care of your customers."

"Was something wrong?"

"Yeah," Griffith said. "When I wanted to change my order, you shoulda told me how good the flapjacks were."

"I tried—"

"Plus you weren't very nice to me," Griffith said. "I like waitresses who are . . . nice."

He tried to put his hand on her hip, and she moved away from him.

"Mister, are you gonna pay for your breakfast?" she asked irritably.

"As a matter of fact," Griffith said, "I ain't— and neither is my friend."

Red looked at Easter, but he looked away in embarrassment.

"Mister," she said to Griffith, "I don't want to have to get the sheriff."

"Go ahead," Griffith said, folding his arms across his chest, "get 'im. We'll wait right here."

Red looked around, confused. Deadbeats usually paid up when she threatened them with the law. She didn't want to have to leave her place unattended to go for the sheriff.

"Of course," Griffith said, "I don't think your local lawman is gonna want to end up planted six feet under over an order of flapjacks, do you?"

She stared at Griffith and said, "You'd kill a man over flapjacks?"

He smiled at her and said, "I killed men for a lot less."

She continued to stare at him in disbelief, and then said, "All right, mister. Forget about paying for breakfast. Just go."

"Go?" he said. "You're tryin' to kick us out?"

"No," she said, "I'm just *asking* you—"

"My friend and I want more coffee," Griffith said stubbornly, "plus you never brought out those biscuits you promised us."

"Coffee," she said, "and biscuits . . ."

"That's right," Griffith said, and then he quickly reached for her and grabbed her wrist before she could move away, "and an apology for not bein' nice. And *then*," he said, stroking her arm with his other hand, "you can show me how nice you can be."

"Let go of me!" she snapped.

"Uh-uh," Griffith said with an ugly smile. "You ain't got a pot of coffee to threaten me with this time, sweetheart."

"Please," she said, "let go—"

From across the room Clint saw that trouble was finally blooming. He got up and walked quickly across to the other table. He got there in time to hear Red ask the man again to please let her go.

"Do what the lady says."

He stood directly behind her and was able to look down at the seated men over her head.

Griffith looked past Red at Clint and frowned. He knew who Clint was and wasn't quite prepared to brace him right there and then, but he also didn't want to back down too easily.

Tim Easter, meanwhile, was looking *very* nervous.

TWELVE

"What are you supposed to be, mister?" Griffith asked. "The boyfriend?"

"No," Clint said, "I'm not the boyfriend. I'm just another customer who doesn't want to see my hostess mistreated."

"Mistreated?" Griffith asked, laughing. "Who's mistreatin' her?"

"The lady asked you to let go of her arm," Clint reminded him.

"Oh," Griffith said and released Red's wrist. This time when she drew it back she rubbed it.

"It's all right, Clint—" she said.

"Now it's time for you and your friend to leave," Clint said, cutting her off.

"Well," Griffith said, licking his lips, "we was plannin' on leavin' anyway."

"Yeah," Easter said, "that's right."

Both men pushed their chairs back and got to their feet, preparing to leave.

"Haven't you forgotten something?" Clint asked.

Both men stopped, and Easter asked nervously,
"Uh, what?"

"Pay the lady for breakfast."

Griffith stiffened. He didn't mind leaving
because they were going to anyway, but now
Clint Adams was trying to get some of his money out of him—money which he had *never* been
prepared to pay anyway.

"Now wait a minute—" he said.

"It's all right, Clint," Red said, turning and
putting her hand on Clint's chest.

"Easy, Red," Clint said. He took hold of her
arm in a much gentler grip than Griffith had
and moved her so that she was standing behind
him.

"Now you listen," Clint told Griffith. "The
lady fed you and put up with your abuse. She's
even willing to let you leave without paying—"

"Well, good, because—"

"But I'm not."

"Hey," Griffith said, as if genuinely puzzled,
"what's with you anyway, mister?"

"The lady is a friend of mine," Clint said. "It
just so happens I look out for my friends."

"Mister, I don't know who you are—" Griffith
started, but Clint cut him off again.

"That's a lie," he said, "but then it doesn't
surprise me that you're also a liar, along with
everything else."

"Hey, now wait a—"

"You know who I am," Clint said. "You recognized me as soon as you walked in, if not earlier. I
don't know from where or when, but that doesn't

matter. I'm telling you this one more time. Pay the lady."

Easter nervously licked his lips and said, "Uh, Jim, don't you think—"

"Shut up," Griffith said. He looked past Clint at Red and asked, "How much do we owe you?"

She told them.

Griffith looked at Easter and said, "Get your money out."

They both counted out their money and handed it to Red, who accepted it tentatively.

"Hey," Clint said as they started to leave.

"Now what?"

"She deserves a tip."

Griffith's face froze, and he looked around the room. The other diners had stopped eating to watch the proceedings.

"You're pushin' it, Adams!"

"You want to push it, friend?" Clint asked.

Griffith stared for a few moments, and although his body didn't move, Clint could sense him mentally backing off a step or two.

"Fifty cents each should be enough."

"*Fifty*—" Easter started, but Griffith stopped him.

"Just leave it on the table, Easter," he said, and dropped four bits on the table himself. Easter followed his example.

"All right?" Griffith asked Clint.

"That's it," Clint said. "You and your friend can leave now."

"Come on," Griffith said to Easter and led the way to the door.

Clint considered shouting after them never to

come back, but he doubted they would.

When they were gone he turned and looked at Red, who was standing with their money held tightly in her clenched fists.

"Hey, relax," he said. "It's all right."

She shook her head and dumped the money onto the table among the dirty dishes and the tip.

"This money wasn't worth you risking yourself, Clint," she said, still shaking her head. "You should have let them leave."

"I did," he said, "but why should they leave without paying? You earned your money."

She closed her eyes, and he saw that she was starting to shake.

"Hey," he said, putting one arm around her shoulders, "come on, come here."

He walked her into the kitchen where they were out of sight of the other diners.

"Red, take it easy," he said, holding her.

"I'm all right," she said, with her face against his chest, "I was just . . . nervous."

"It's all right."

She lifted her head and looked up at him.

"How did those men know who you are?" she asked. "Are you . . . somebody?"

He laughed. He'd never been asked that question in quite that way before.

"I like to think I'm somebody."

She banged her fist on his chest lightly and said, "You know what I mean."

"I have a little bit of a reputation," he said, grossly understating the fact, "in some parts of the country."

"A little bit?" she asked.

"Don't worry about it," he said. "Are you all right, now?"

"Yes," she said, "yes, I'm fine. I have customers to see to."

"Do you want me to stay and help you?"

She pushed away from him and smoothed her apron over her thighs.

"No, no," she said, "that's silly. You can't work in a restaurant."

"And why not?"

"Because," she said, looking him right in the eye, "you're somebody—and not somebody who should be cleaning or waiting tables."

"What's the matter with waiting tables?" he asked her. "It's good, honest work."

She stared at him and said, "Is that what you have a reputation for? Good, honest work?"

He frowned.

"I have a reputation more for things I did years ago than for things I've done recently, Red," he said. "Recently I'd say yeah, my reputation would be for being honest."

She stared at him for a few moments and then said, "I don't think I could ever believe anything bad of you, Clint. Not after what you did for me out there."

"That was nothing," he said. "They weren't ready to fight over the price of a meal."

"They were with me," she said, "but they weren't with you. That was the difference."

They stared at each other for a few moments, and then it was as if she suddenly remembered that she had a business to run.

"I—I have to go back to work," she said.

"Uh-huh," he said. "I have some things I have to do also."

"Will I . . . see you later? For lunch, I mean."

"Unless you know a better place to eat in town."

She smiled and said, "I don't know a better place to eat in the *West*."

"That's what I like," he said, "a woman with confidence."

THIRTEEN

For several reasons Clint decided to go right from Red's to the sheriff's office. Just in case the two men decided to make a complaint against him, he wanted to make sure the sheriff had his side of the story. He also wanted to let the man know he was in town. It was sort of a courtesy call. After all, he did have his reputation to live down—as opposed to most men, who tried to live up to theirs—and he wanted the sheriff to be aware that not only was he in town, but that he himself had brought it to the man's attention. In that way, he was letting the law know that he wasn't looking for any trouble.

He found the office. Sometimes there was a sign outside the sheriff's office announcing the name of the local lawman, but that was not the case with the Gambler's Fork sheriff. Clint knocked on the door and entered.

The man sitting behind the desk was wearing a badge, but it was a deputy's badge. He appeared to be in his twenties, very lean, and probably very tall, when he was standing.

"Help ya?" he asked.

"I was looking for the sheriff."

"He's out right now," the young man said. "My name's Blaine. I'm the deputy."

"My name's Clint Adams, Deputy," Clint said. "Does that name ring a bell with you?"

Apparently it did. Recognition was plain on the man's face, and he quickly got to his feet, as if he wasn't quite sure what to do.

"I—I know who you are, sir," he said nervously.

"Take it easy, son," Clint said. "I'm just here to let the sheriff know that I'm in town. As a courtesy, you know?"

"A—a courtesy?"

"That's right," Clint said. "I'm staying over at the hotel, if he wants to talk to me later."

"Uh . . . which hotel? We got two."

"Oh, that's right," Clint said. "Well, I don't know the name of it. It's the one nearest the livery stable."

"I'll—I'll tell him."

"Okay," Clint said. "Thanks."

He walked to the door and opened it, then turned to ask the deputy another question.

"By the way, what's the sheriff's name?"

"It's, uh, Carver," Deputy Blaine said, "Joe Carver—uh, Sheriff Joe Carver."

"Well, you tell Sheriff Joe Carver that I was here to pay a courtesy call."

"Uh, sure, Mr. Adams," Blaine said. "I'll tell 'im. Uh, courtesy call."

"Thanks, Deputy," Clint said and left.

When Clint Adams left the sheriff's office, Jeff Blaine remained standing, staring at the door for a few moments. That was the *Gunsmith* for Christ's sake! He'd heard the name for a long time but never thought he'd actually get to meet the man. And he'd acted like such an ass! Some deputy he was.

Slowly, he sat back down, and then he took a huge deep breath and let it out in a rush. He hadn't known what to do or how to act when he'd heard the name Clint Adams, and he knew he'd acted like a damned fool. Sheriff Carver wouldn't have been so nervous—or even if he was, he wouldn't have showed it.

Abruptly, Blaine jumped up again and reached for his hat. This was something he had to find the sheriff and tell him about right away.

FOURTEEN

Clint was relaxing in his hotel room when he heard a knock on the door. If it was the sheriff, he thought, the man made good time.

When he opened the door, he was surprised. It wasn't the sheriff. The only other person it had occurred to him it might have been was Red, only she would have had to leave her business to come over. He sure hadn't expected a bald-headed man who looked like he was chiseled out of stone.

"Help you?" Clint asked.

"Mr. Clint Adams?"

"That's right."

"My name is Jenkins, sir," the man said. "I work for Mr. Bartock."

"Ah," Clint said.

"Mr. Bartock would like to extend to you the offer of transportation to his ranch later."

"Is he making the same offer to the other players who have arrived?"

"Yes, sir."

"Would it be all right if I rode my own horse out there?"

"Certainly, sir."

The man's subservient manner did not fit him, as far as Clint was concerned. He felt sure that this Jenkins was much more than just a servant.

"I don't want to insult my host—"

"That is not an issue, sir," Jenkins said. "You may ride your own horse with no danger of that. Should the others accept our offer, you may follow along or ride out at your leisure. Dinner will be served at six."

"When will your transportation be leaving town?"

"At exactly five o'clock," Jenkins said. "If you would like to go out to the ranch prior to that, you would be very welcome."

"I see," Clint said.

"There is also the question of your living quarters while you are here for the game," Jenkins said. "You may stay in town or at the ranch. There are rooms available for all the players."

"Even if we all decide to stay?"

"Yes, sir."

"Must I make that decision now?"

"Of course not," Jenkins said. "Tonight, after dinner, Mr. Bartock will make the offer. That is when you may accept or decline."

"Well, I'll think about it between now and then," Clint said. "Thank you, Mr. Jenkins."

"No," the bald-headed man said, "not 'Mister' Jenkins, sir. Just Jenkins."

"All right," Clint said. "Thank you, Jenkins."

The man executed a very slight bow and started away.

"Excuse me," Clint said.

"Yes?" Jenkins stopped in the hall and turned to face him.

"How many other players are already in town?"

"Three," Jenkins said.

"Did you make the same offer to them?"

"Yes, sir."

"Did they accept?"

"Yes, sir."

"Where will you be leaving from," Clint asked, "if I decide to ride along?"

"The other three gentlemen are staying at the other hotel, sir," Jenkins said. "We will be leaving from in front of that location."

"Makes sense," Clint said with a nod. "All right, thank you."

"Yes, sir."

Jenkins turned, continued down the hall, and descended the stairs. Clint backed into his room and closed the door, then walked to the window and looked down at the street. Moments later Jenkins appeared, crossing the street and walking away until he was out of sight.

Clint might have accepted the offer of transportation, but he did not want to leave Duke in town while he was out at the ranch, just in case he did decide to stay out there for the duration of the game.

Jenkins had approached Cort Mason first with his offer, and then in succession Tim Easter and

Jim Griffith. Griffith had asked him the names of the other players in the game.

"You will find that out tonight, at dinner," Jenkins had said.

"I want to know now," Griffith had said, almost petulantly.

"I am not at liberty to say right now, Mr. Griffith," Jenkins had said, turning and walking away from the man's door.

Once he had visited all four of the players who had arrived, Jenkins went to arrange for a buggy to take three of them—Mason, Griffith, and Easter—out to the ranch later on that evening.

Both Mason and Clint Adams had been exactly what Jenkins had expected. However, Griffith and Easter had been exactly what he'd been afraid of.

FIFTEEN

Clint was sitting in a chair in front of the hotel contemplating lunch when he saw the man with the badge crossing the street toward him. This time it was not the deputy, but the sheriff himself.

"Sheriff," he said as the man started past him into the hotel.

"Yes?"

Clint stood.

"I think you might be looking for me."

The sheriff turned to face him. He was a big man, built wide but with the height to carry it. He appeared to be in his mid-thirties.

"I am if you're Clint Adams."

"I am."

"Sheriff Joe Carver, Mr. Adams," the man said, extending his hand. "I'm sorry I wasn't in my office when you came to make your courtesy call. I wanted to thank you in person for it."

"That's all right," Clint said. The man had a firm handshake, and he released Clint's hand without initiating a test of strength. "I just like to make the local law aware of the fact that I'm in town."

"It makes a difference," the sheriff said. He looked around, spotted another chair, and asked, "Mind if I sit a spell?"

"No," Clint said, "pull the chair over."

Carver retrieved the other chair and put it next to Clint's, and the two men sat down.

"Would you care to tell me why you're in Gambler's Fork?"

"I thought everyone knew that already," Clint said, "or at least assumed that they knew."

Carver smiled. He had a smooth, clean shaven face. Clint wondered at a man in his mid-thirties who had the skin of an eighteen-year-old.

"I don't like to assume anything," Carver said, "when I can go to the source and ask."

"Sound decision," Clint said. "All right, I'm here for Harry Bartock's game."

Carver nodded, as if he'd known that all along and Clint had simply confirmed it.

"I guess that means there are some other players in town who *haven't* made courtesy calls."

"I had a visit from a man named Jenkins this morning," Clint said.

"That one," Carver said. "That's a strange man, Mr. Adams."

"Clint, please," he said. "I think I know what you mean, Sheriff. He looks like more than just a manservant or a butler."

"Oh, he is," Carver said. "I think Mr. Jenkins might just be the strongest man I've ever met—

and I'm no slouch when it comes to strength, Mis—Clint. I mean, I'm six five and he's what—five eight? I'm not sure I could match him in brute strength."

"You've never had an opportunity to put it to the test, eh?"

"No," Carver said, "and I hope I never do. What did he say?"

"That there were three other players in town. He was offering us all transportation."

"Did you accept?"

"I prefer to ride my own horse."

Carver nodded.

"Tell me something," Clint said.

"If I can."

"This kind of game is pretty big," he said, "lots of money going back and forth. What kind of security does Bartock have?"

"Private," Carver said. "I've been sheriff here for eight years, before the games started. When he first bought his ranch and started building it up, he made it clear to me that he had his own security. During the games he just increases it."

"I see."

"I've, uh, never been to his house—inside, I mean. I understand he's a gracious host, but this game is the only time that he ever allows guests. He's a very private man, Clint. Eccentric, you might say."

"I see."

"And young," Carver said. "You'll be surprised to know he's not yet thirty."

"That does surprise me," Clint admitted.

"Where did he make his money?"

"I sure don't know," Carver said, "and he's never volunteered the information. He's got plenty of it, though, I can tell you that."

"I wonder why he chose to settle here?"

"Don't know that, either," Carver said. "In fact, I know very little about the man, and that's the way he likes to keep it."

"Well . . . it sounds like it could be an interesting game."

"Oh, I'm sure of that," Carver said. "Well, I've got to go and do my job. I'll find those other players and just welcome them to town."

And acquaint himself with who they are, Clint thought. Carver struck him as a good lawman.

He stood with the man and shook hands again.

"Again, thanks for the visit," Carver said. "It would make my job a hell of a lot simpler if strangers in town would call on me instead of making me look for them."

"I bet it would, Sheriff," Clint said.

"Good luck at the game, Clint." Carver stepped into the street and began to cross.

Clint was impressed with Carver. He'd seen more then his share of local law who only saw the job as a way to make some extra money, wear a badge, and have people respect you. Too many of them never did anything to *deserve* the respect.

Sheriff Joe Carver was one of the few who did.

SIXTEEN

Clint had lunch at Red's, arriving there after one o'clock.

"I was expecting you earlier," she said.

"I had a long, leisurely breakfast, remember," he said, smiling.

"Yes," she said, "and eventful. I remember. I want to thank you again for what you did."

He waved her thanks away.

"What's good for lunch?" he asked.

"That depends," she replied. "Are you coming back for dinner?"

"Uh, no, I can't," he said. "I have to . . . be somewhere tonight."

"Ah," she said, "dinner at the ranch, huh?"

He looked up at her and asked, "Do you know Harry Bartock, Red?"

"I've met him," she said. "Once or twice."

"Were you impressed?"

"I don't know," she said. "Was I supposed to be?"

"I don't know, either," he said. "I guess I'll

64

tell you after I meet him. Anyway, what do you suggest for dinner?"

"I have some beef stew I think you'll like," she said. "And I've made some fresh rolls."

"Sounds good," he said. "Bring it on."

When he had arrived practically every table was occupied, but when she returned with his lunch some of the people had left and gone on with their day's work. Consequently she had some time to sit and talk to him.

"How is it?" she asked, after his first taste.

"It's delicious," he said honestly.

"I don't know what you'll be eating for dinner tonight," she said, "but I'd be curious to find out how it tastes."

"By comparison, you mean?"

"Well, yes," she said shyly. "You know, you asked me if I've ever met Mr. Bartock. Truth of the matter is, I've met his cook more than I've met him. I usually run into her at the general store."

"Is she any good?"

"If I knew that," she said, "I wouldn't be asking you to tell me. She's very nice, but I don't know what kind of cook she is. All I know is that she makes a lot more money than I do cooking."

"Well," Clint said, "I don't see how she could be a better cook than you. Your food is better than what I've eaten in San Francisco and New York."

Her eyes brightened considerably at the mention of these cities.

"Have you been to many fancy restaurants in those cities?" she asked.

"Some, yes."

"That's what I'd like to do," she said, folding her arms onto the table and leaning on them. "I want to cook for one of those fancy restaurants."

"I don't see why you couldn't," he said.

She made a face and said, "Getting there is more the problem. I'm trying to save money, but it isn't easy."

"It never is," he said.

She looked at him, then shook her head and looked away. Obviously, she had been about to say something and changed her mind.

"What were you going to say?" he asked.

"Oh, nothing . . ."

"Come on, Red . . ."

"Oh, just that you must have a lot of money if you're playing in the big poker game. What would you know about having to scrimp and save?"

"Believe me," he said, "I've gone through hard times myself, mostly when I was younger."

"What about your . . . reputation?" she asked. "Do you make a lot of money doing what . . . you do?"

"No," he said, "but I *have* saved over the years, which is why when an opportunity like this comes up, I can take it."

"I suppose so," she said. "Who am I to judge? I still don't know what you do."

"I'm a gunsmith, Red."

"A gunsmith?" she said. "You mean . . . you repair guns?"

"Repair them, modify then, build them," he

said. "I like working with them."

"And can you use a gun?"

He hesitated just a moment and then said, "Yes."

"Well?"

"Very well."

She studied him for a moment, as if trying to read between the lines of what he was saying.

"All right," he said, putting down his utensils, "since you're so curious—"

"No, no," she said, holding up her hands, "it's all right, you don't have to talk about it if you don't want to."

"Just be quiet and listen," he said. "The reputation I have is not for buildings guns or repairing them, it's for using them."

"You mean . . . like a gunman?"

"Yes, exactly like that," he said. "I was labeled at a time in my youth when it appealed to me. It wasn't until I reached my thirties that I realized what a . . . fool I had been to encourage it. By then it was too late. It's been something I've had to live with, and now that I'm older I still carry it with me."

She was silent for a few moments while he continued to eat.

"It must be terrible," she said finally, "to have to keep paying your whole life for something you did when you were young."

"It's not so bad, I guess," he said. "I try to keep a low profile."

"Oh, I see!" she said, as something suddenly occurred to her. "That's what you meant this morning, by saying that those men knew who you were."

"Yes," he said. "I knew as soon as they walked in that they recognized me."

"So you knew they wouldn't go against you when you made them pay?"

"Well, I didn't *know* that," he said, "but I was hoping. I didn't think they were prepared right at that moment to try me."

"So . . . it was really your reputation that did all the work this morning?"

"You could say that, yes," he said. "I have to admit, *sometimes* it comes in handy and keeps me from having to get into a fight, but more times than not somebody—usually somebody young—will recognize me and decide he wants to make a big rep for himself."

"And then you have to fight?"

"Yes."

"And . . . kill?"

"Sometimes," he said. "Sometimes it's either kill or get killed. Given a choice like that, there's only one way to go."

"I see . . ."

There was an awkward silence while she digested all that he had told her.

"This stew is really good," he said finally, unable to think of anything else to say.

"Would you like some more?"

"No," he said, "if I'm going to judge this cook of Bartock's, I'd better not stuff myself."

"How about some coffee?"

"Sure," he said.

"I'll get it."

She got up and went into the kitchen. He wiped the bowl clean with the last roll and then sat and waited for her, thinking.

In spite of the fact that his kind of life must have been alien to her, she didn't seem particularly shocked or disgusted by what he'd told her, although she *had* thought about it quite a bit. He was glad she hadn't been put off. He liked her, which was why he'd decided to be honest with her. Actually, he'd opened his mouth and the truth just seemed to pour out of it.

She was an uncommon woman, one he found himself wanting to be liked by.

SEVENTEEN

Clint decided ahead of time that he would stay out at the ranch during the game. It made more sense than going to and from town all the time. If he changed his mind, he could always return and check back into the hotel. For now, he checked out of the hotel, then walked over to the livery for Duke.

His timing was perfect; when he rode up to the other hotel there was already a buggy out front, with Jenkins sitting up on it. There was a roan horse tied to the back of the buggy, presumably the animal Jenkins had ridden into town.

When Jenkins had come to Clint's room earlier in the day, he had been dressed in the same black suit he was wearing now, with a white shirt, but he had not been wearing the hat—a bowler hat. Clint had seen many of them when he was in England—and a few in San Francisco and New York—but he hadn't seen one for quite a while.

He rode up to the buggy and looked down at

Jenkins. The man turned his head and showed no
surprise at seeing Clint, but he did show some
interest in Duke.

"My word," he said, "what a magnificent animal."

"Thanks."

"I can understand why you would prefer to
ride him to the ranch rather than leaving him
in town."

"Where are the others?" Clint asked.

"They should be here at any moment," Jenkins
said.

As he spoke, a man approached them from the
street, behind Clint. Jenkins looked past Clint,
who turned in his saddle and saw that it was
Sheriff Carver.

"Mr. Adams."

"Sheriff."

"Getting ready to go out to the ranch, I see."

"That's right."

"Hello, Jenkins."

"Good day, Sheriff," Jenkins said. His face was
expressionless, his eyes flat and cold, as was his
tone of voice. Clint realized in that moment that
Jenkins disliked either Joe Carver or what he
represented.

"How's your boss?" Carver asked.

"Mr. Bartock is quite well, thank you."

"Haven't seen him in town in some time,"
Carver commented.

"That is true," was all Jenkins would say.

"You all set for the game out there?" Carver
asked. "Security-wise, I mean."

"Yes," Jenkins said, "we are quite prepared, Sheriff . . . for anything."

"Well, that's good to hear," Carver said. "Wouldn't want there to be any trouble out there."

"We will do our best," Jenkins said, "to see that there is no need to disturb you, Sheriff."

Carver stared hard at Jenkins, who refused to look away, and said, "I'll appreciate that, Jenkins."

He looked away from Jenkins then and looked at Clint.

"Good luck out there."

"Thanks, Sheriff."

Carver gave Jenkins another long look, then turned and walked away. Clint noticed that Jenkins watched until the sheriff disappeared down the street.

"Why do I get the feeling," Clint said, "that you and the sheriff will never be best friends?"

"You are a very perceptive man, Mr. Adams," Jenkins said.

"Is there any particular reason *why* you two don't get along?"

"It's very simple, really," Jenkins said. "We don't like one another."

"Yes," Clint said, "but *why*—I mean, if I'm not being too nosy?"

Jenkins looked at Clint and was about to answer when a man came out of the hotel.

EIGHTEEN

Jenkins stepped down from the buggy to greet the man formally.

"Ah, Mr. Mason."

Clint had never seen the man before, but he'd heard of him.

"Cort Mason," he said.

Mason looked up at him and said, "Do I know you?"

"No," Clint said, "but I've heard of you."

"Mr. Mason," Jenkins said, making the introductions, "this is Mr. Clint Adams. He will also be playing in the game."

"Really?" Mason said. "Clint Adams?"

"That's right."

Mason climbed into the back of the buggy and before making himself comfortable on the leather seats reached out to shake hands with Clint, who had to back Duke up a few feet to do so.

"This should be an interesting game," Mason said. "I'm aware of your reputation—with cards, I mean."

"I wasn't aware that I had one."

"In certain circles you do," Mason said. "I have played on occasion with both Luke Short and Bat Masterson. They speak very highly of your, uh, talents."

"*They're* talented," Clint said. "I just get lucky sometimes."

"Nothing wrong with luck," Mason said, shaking his head. "It's carried me through my share of hard times, believe me."

"Here come our other two players," Jenkins said.

Clint looked away from Mason toward the hotel and saw the two men come out. He recognized them immediately. They did not see him right away because of the buggy.

"Mr. Cort Mason," Jenkins said, introducing Mason first, "these are Mr. James Griffith and Mr. Timothy Easter."

"Gentlemen," Mason said, touching the brim of his hat in greeting.

"I heard of you, Mason," Griffith said. "You're supposed to be pretty good."

"You'll find out soon enough," Mason said.

"And this is Clint Adams," Jenkins said.

Clint moved Duke away from the buggy so both men could see him clearly. Griffith narrowed his eyes, and Easter just stared.

"We've met," Clint said.

"Oh really?" Jenkins asked. "Recently?"

"This morning," Clint said, "at breakfast."

"I see," Jenkins said. He looked back and forth from Clint to the other men and felt there was definitely tension in the air.

"Gentlemen," he said to Griffith and Easter, "if you'll climb aboard, we'll be off."

"What about the other players?" Griffith asked. "Ain't there more players?"

"Two more," Jenkins said, "but they are not in town. One would assume that they will come directly to the ranch—if they are not there already."

Griffith and Easter climbed into the buggy and sat on the seat opposite Cort Mason. Mason, too, felt the tension in the air between the two men and Clint Adams. Maybe later, he thought, he'd ask Clint about it.

Jenkins climbed aboard and picked up the reins.

"Very well, gentlemen," he said, "we're off."

"We're *off*?" Griffith repeated.

"What's that mean?" Easter asked.

"It means," Mason said, "we're on our way to the ranch."

"Oh," Easter said, "well, it's about time. I want to get started playin'."

Cort Mason studied the two men across from him. He prided himself on being able to size up his competition fairly quickly, and he did not see either of these men as a challenge. Of course, he'd reserve his final decision until they were actually sitting across from each other at the poker table. For now, though, he saw Clint Adams as the only real threat to him.

For his part Clint Adams was not happy with the presence of Griffith and Easter. He preferred *not* to play poker with men he didn't like or respect, or with whom he'd had some sort of . . . confrontation. It changed the nature of the game. He had come too far to play in this game, however, and he wasn't about to start making demands regarding who would play and who would not.

Jenkins had many duties in Harry Bartock's household, but the overriding one—especially during the game—was security. There was obviously a problem between Clint Adams and the two men, Griffith and Easter. He felt that this was due to the fact that they had been forced—in an effort to fill the game—to extend invitations to men of their *type*. It did not bother him that they toiled on the wrong side of the law. There had been many such men in and out of Bartock's game. In the past, however, *they* had all been men of a certain . . . class. These men, Jenkins felt, had very little or no class whatsoever.

He would be keeping a close eye on them throughout the game.

NINETEEN

The ride out to the Bartock ranch was uneventful. Clint rode behind the buggy and noticed that Cort Mason did not engage in conversation with Griffith and Easter. In fact, there was no conversation between anyone the entire way, until they came to within sight of the ranch.

"Is that it?" Griffith called out to Jenkins.

Clint heard him so he assumed that when Jenkins did not reply it was by design.

"Hey!" Griffith called, and when Jenkins still did not reply, the man gave up.

Before long they were in front of the house. Clint was quite impressed. The house was huge, larger than any ranch house he had ever seen before—and he had been on some big spreads in the past. This, though, was something truly special.

The grounds were nothing extraordinary; the barn, the bunkhouse, it was all in keeping with a working ranch, but the house was incredible. The white pillars in the front made it look like a mansion on a Louisiana plantation.

The front door—three times the size of any door Clint had ever seen—opened, and a man stepped out. If Sheriff Carver had not told Clint that Bartock was not yet thirty, Clint might have assumed that he was a man in his early twenties. However, he took "not yet thirty" to mean that the man was closer to twenty-eight or -nine.

Clint dismounted, and a man quickly appeared to take Duke from him.

"Take good care of him," Clint said.

"Don't worry, mister," the man said, casting an approving look at Duke. "I know good horseflesh when I see it."

There was no porch, only two wide steps from the ground to the door. Clint thought the area in front of the house was called a "portico," although he wasn't sure. He simply had never spent much time around homes this grand.

"I don't believe it," Tim Easter said, probably speaking for everyone. "This is your *house*?"

"Mr. Bartock," Jenkins said, "Mr. James Griffith, Mr. Timothy Easter, Mr. Cort Mason, and Mr. Clint Adams."

"Gentlemen," Harry Bartock said, spreading his arms wide, "welcome to my home."

He stepped forward and shook hands with each man in turn. He lingered in front of Clint, holding his hand a touch longer than the others'.

"It's a true pleasure to have you all here," he said, but he was looking directly at Clint when he said it. He was obviously more impressed with having the Gunsmith at his home but did not want to show favoritism in front of the others. Finally, he released Clint's hand and stepped back.

"Let's go inside, please," he announced. "Dinner will be ready soon. We can have drinks, and I will introduce you to the fifth player."

"Another one showed up?" Griffith asked. "Good. I was afraid we was gonna be short."

"No," Bartock said, "we are not short a player, Mr. Griffith. The fifth arrived about an hour ago, and we are still expecting a sixth. Please, come inside. Jenkins!"

"Yes, sir." Jenkins led the way inside.

They followed single file, Clint second from the rear, with Bartock right behind him.

"Jenkins," Bartock said when they were inside, "take everyone to the dining room, please. I will fetch our other guest from the den."

"Yes, sir. This way, please . . ." Jenkins said, but all four of the guests were craning their necks, taking in the huge foyer and the high, ornate ceiling.

"I have never seen anything like this before," Clint said, obviously awed.

"Yes," Jenkins said, "Mr. Bartock is very proud of this house. He designed it himself."

"Impressive," Clint said, understating the case.

"Wow," Easter said.

"Shit." Griffith whistled.

"This way, please?" Jenkins said again.

He pointed the way and waited while each man passed him in turn, and then he followed.

"The dining room is that way," he said, pointing and then taking the lead.

When they reached the dining room, they took the time to look around again. Clint noticed the table, which was easily the longest table he had ever seen. He remembered what the sheriff had said about Bartock not having guests, and imagined the man sitting at this table alone, having his meals.

"Gentlemen," Bartock said, entering the room from behind them, "allow me to introduce my fifth guest."

From behind him a woman entered the room, and all five of the men in the room—including Jenkins—stopped to stare at her.

"Gentlemen," Bartock said, "Miss Paula Harrison."

TWENTY

"Hello, gentlemen," Paula Harrison said.

Harry Bartock was amused at the reaction of the other men.

"I have to admit that I was pretty surprised myself," Bartock told them. "After all, I had made a mistake and was expecting a *Paul* Harrison. To my surprise, *Miss* Harrison arrived announcing herself as a player in my game."

"A woman?" Griffith said. "You're gonna let a woman play in the game?"

"Of course I am," Bartock said. "After all, she was invited."

"How could you invite her?" Griffith asked. "You didn't even know who she was."

"She was recommended," Bartock said, "highly. That I did not know she was a woman was my error, and no one else's."

"Well," Cort Mason said, stepping forward, "I for one am delighted that I will not only be able to play poker, but also have the opportunity to look at someone beautiful while I'm doing it."

"Thank you," Paula Harrison said.

She was tall, probably five nine, with long auburn hair that was, at the moment, gathered up over her head. Clint had no doubt that if she let it loose it would tumble down well past her shoulders. She was wearing a green evening dress, having obviously dressed for dinner. It revealed her smooth shoulders and upper arms, and just an enticing glimpse of cleavage.

"And while you're looking at me," she went on, speaking to Mason, "maybe I'll be taking your money."

Mason started to laugh, but when he saw that she was *not* laughing he stopped and said, "Oh, I'm sorry. You were being serious, weren't you?"

She pointedly ignored him *and* the question and turned her attention to Clint.

"And what about you, Mr. Adams?" she asked. "Do you see anything wrong with a woman playing in the game?"

"Not at all," he said. "I've played in many games with women, and for the most part they were excellent poker players—better than a lot of men I've played against."

"Thank you for the vote of confidence," she said, gracing him with a smile.

"Jenkins," Bartock said, "get the gentlemen drinks. Miss Harrison, another glass of sherry?"

"No, thank you, Mr. Bartock," she said. "Perhaps after dinner."

"Of course," Bartock said. "Please, be seated at the table, over here by me."

He walked her to the table, held a chair out for her, and then sat at the head of the table with her to his left.

Jenkins took drink orders from the men and went off to fill them.

"Mr. Adams?" Bartock called. "Would you sit here, on my right?"

And across from Paula Harrison, Clint thought.

"Of course," he said, taking the offered seat.

"Gentlemen?" Bartock said. "Will you all be seated?"

"What about the last player?" Griffith asked. He was annoyed because Cort Mason had gotten the seat next to Paula Harrison.

"Don't worry," Bartock said. "He'll be here."

Jenkins returned carrying a tray of drinks and gave each man the drink of his preference. Griffith and Easter had whiskey while Clint and Mason went for Bartock's offer of sherry.

The conversation was trivial, because there were just too many people there for any other kind. Clint felt sure that Bartock would rather have talked to him or Mason—or Miss Harrison—without Griffith and Easter around. Since he had invited them, though, he was forced to play host to everyone.

Clint himself would certainly have rather talked with Paula Harrison than any of the others. Bartock was his host, however, so he showed him the respect of listening to his chatter.

Jenkins was in and out. The man always seemed to know when Bartock was going to need him, and he would appear. At one point he came in to announce that dinner was about to be served.

"Very good, Jenkins," Bartock said. "I'm sure we're all very hungry."

"I could eat," Griffith said, "but I'd rather play cards. Tell me about the game, Bartock—"

"*Mister* Bartock," Jenkins said, staring hard at Griffith.

Griffith stared back, but he wasn't able to maintain eye contact and eventually looked away.

"Okay, *Mister* Bartock," he said, "about the game—"

"We will discuss the game after dinner, Mr. Griffith," Bartock said.

"I just want to know—"

Firmly, without raising his voice, Bartock said, "*After* dinner, sir."

Griffith looked around and found himself the center of attention. He didn't like it.

"Okay," he said, "so we'll talk after we eat. . . ."

Bartock looked up at Jenkins and said, "Tell Cook to serve dinner, Jenkins."

TWENTY-ONE

During dinner Clint decided that Bartock had apparently had a change of heart. He acted as if Griffith and Easter weren't worth his time and directed most of his conversation to Paula Harrison, Cort Mason, and Clint. He was probably figuring that if the other two men wanted to play badly enough, they wouldn't get offended and leave. And even if they did, they'd still have five for the game.

He talked with Mason for a while, catching up with what the man had been doing since he'd last played in this game a couple of years ago.

"I had about an hour to talk with Miss Harrison before you all arrived," Bartock said.

"Lucky man," Mason said.

"Yes," Bartock said, then looked at Clint. "She was recommended to this game by a friend of yours, Mr. Adams."

"Oh? Who was that?"

"Ben Thompson."

Clint knew Thompson, who had an equal reputation with a gun and a deck of cards, but he wouldn't have called them friends. He decided not to point that out, though.

"How do you know Ben?" Clint asked Paula.

"We've dealt in the same houses," she said.

"Ah, then you're a dealer."

"I have been," she said. "For the past few years, though, I've preferred to play for myself."

Clint studied her for a moment. Initially he had figured her for her late twenties, but he revised his estimate upward about five years now. Late twenties or early thirties, however, she was still an extraordinary-looking woman.

"How do you like the dinner?" Bartock asked Clint suddenly.

"Oh," Clint said, "it's fine—very good, in fact."

Bartock had had the cook prepare a whole game bird for each of them, stuffed with wild rice and garnished with vegetables.

"I suspect, since you have been in town since yesterday, that you've eaten at Red's?"

Clint looked at Bartock and wondered if the man knew or was guessing.

"Yes, as a matter of fact, I have," Clint said.

"Ah, then you no doubt agree that her cooking is better than the fare here tonight."

"Well . . ."

"Yes, yes," Bartock said, "as a good guest you don't want to say that, but there it is. I know that for a fact because I have tasted Red's cooking myself. Not for some time, admittedly, but I doubt that her talent has faded any."

"No," Clint said, "I can't say I think it has. I

found her food to be excellent—possibly the best I've ever had."

"Yes, I agree," Bartock said. "You know, when I first came here and tasted her cooking, I offered her a job cooking for me. She turned me down. Said she preferred running her own place. I admire her for that."

"She sounds like a special woman," Paula Harrison said, looking at the two men. "I'd like to meet her—and I'd certainly like to taste her cooking."

"Perhaps you should," Bartock said, "maybe for breakfast or lunch tomorrow . . . depending on how long the game goes before we take a break."

"That sounds like we're gonna start tonight," Jim Griffith spoke up from down the table.

Bartock frowned, but then decided to answer the man.

"Yes, Mr. Griffith, the game will begin at eleven p.m. tonight."

"Well, good," Griffith said. "Will that be with or without the other player?"

"I have already told you not to worry about that," Bartock said. "The other player will be here shortly, I'm sure."

"And who would the other player be?" Cort Mason asked. "You've never said, and I find myself becoming very curious."

"I imagine you are," Bartock said, "but I'd like to save the identity of the other player until later, when I make the introductions."

"Now I'm curious as well," Paula Harrison said.

"I think we all are," Clint said. "I think that's Mr. Bartock's intention."

"A little game," Bartock said, spreading his hands. "Please forgive me. You'll know the answer very soon, I'm sure."

Clint looked across the table at Paula Harrison, who shrugged.

"Are we all finished?" Bartock asked. "Good. We'll have coffee and dessert in the den."

Jenkins appeared just at that moment, and Bartock informed him of this.

"Very good, sir," Jenkins said. "I will bring it in."

"Shall we go into the den?" Bartock asked the others. "Miss Harrison, you know the way. If you would be so kind?"

"Of course," she said.

As they stood, Cort Mason, being the closest to the woman, offered her his arm, which she accepted. They walked on ahead, with Griffith and Easter behind them. Bartock fell into step next to Clint.

"I've been wanting to tell you how delighted I am that you accepted my invitation this year."

"I've been kind of busy in the past."

"Oh, I understand that," Bartock said. "I just wanted you to know that you are the only person I have invited every single year."

"I'm flattered."

"That is why I am especially pleased that you were able to attend this year. I'm just sorry that the . . . quality of our players is not quite up to standards this time."

"That's not your fault."

"Jenkins tells me that you had an . . . altercation with Mr. Griffith and Mr. Easter?"

"It wasn't much," Clint said. "They were giving Red a hard time at breakfast and then didn't want to pay her. I made sure they did."

"I see," Bartock said. "Do you believe that the hard feelings will carry over to the poker table?"

"It's possible that it will on their part," Clint said, "but not on mine. I intend to play my game."

"Excellent," Bartock said. "I was hoping you'd say that. Now that you're here, I want to see your best game."

"I always play my best game, Mr. Bartock."

"When we're not with the others, Mr. Adams," Bartock said, "I wish you would call me Harry. Actually, I should admit that I'm quite a fan of yours."

"A fan?"

"Oh yes," Bartock said. "I think I've read everything that's ever been written about you."

"About seventy-five percent of that stuff is made up," he said.

"I realize that, of course," Bartock said, "but even twenty-five percent of it is quite amazing, don't you agree?"

Clint didn't, but he replied with a noncommittal nod.

TWENTY-TWO

They were in the den when Jenkins came in carrying a tray of coffee. Behind him was another man, this one wearing a gun. He was also carrying a tray, and on it were slices of pie. Clint assumed that this was one of Bartock's security force. Right now, though, he was carrying peach pie.

Everyone took a piece of pie except for Jim Griffith. He did, however, take a cup of coffee.

"It's nine p.m.," Bartock said while his guests ate their desserts. "We have two hours before the game begins. I would ask you now how many of you intend to stay on the premises for the duration of the game?"

One by one they replied, all in the affirmative.

"Good," Bartock said, "very good. It will make everything easier. Meals will be served at certain times of the day. Jenkins will supply you with those times."

"And if we want to eat at some other time?" Griffith asked.

Bartock looked at him and said, "Then you will have to find someplace else to eat. My cook will not be on call twenty-four hours a day."

"That's understandable," Cort Mason said.

"Water will be available to you at all times," Bartock told them. "There are bathtubs in all the rooms."

"Really?" Easter said, the only one who was surprised.

Bartock waited a beat and then said, "Yes . . . really.

"For those of you who did not bring your own horses, our horses will be available to you whenever you wish to take a ride," Bartock went on.

"Good," Paula Harrison said. "Horseback riding clears my mind."

"My men will saddle a horse for you, or you may pick out your own. Is all of this understood?"

They all agreed that it was.

"All right," Bartock said. "Later you'll all see the room we'll be playing in. This is very important. No one will be allowed in that room when the game is suspended."

"Wait a minute," Griffith said. "We can take our money, right?"

"No."

"What?"

"We will be playing with chips," Bartock said, "and no one cashes out until the end of the game— and I mean when the game is *over*. When we take breaks, all of the chips will be left on the table."

"Oh no," Griffith said. "When I leave that room my money goes with me."

"There will be security on the room at all times," Bartock said. "Your money will be safe."

"My money goes where I go," Griffith said.

Bartock stared at Griffith for a long time and then looked at each of the other players—or *would-be* players—in turn.

"Does anyone else object to the house rules?"

"I don't," Mason said, "but then I've played here before."

"Mr. Adams?" Bartock said.

"I don't like it," Clint said, "but if it's a house rule, I can live with it."

"Miss Harrison?"

"It's fine with me."

"Mr. Easter?"

Easter swallowed hard and looked from Bartock to Griffith.

"Forget it," Griffith said. "If everyone else is gonna go along with it, I will, too."

"Mr. Easter?" Bartock said.

"Uh, sure, I'll go along with it."

"Very good."

"How about your mystery player?" Griffith said. "Is he gonna object?"

"If he does," Bartock said, spreading his hands, "then we won't play."

They all exchanged glances and then waited for the next set of instructions.

"All right," Bartock said, setting down his empty coffee cup, "does anyone have any questions about anything I've said?"

There were no questions, although Griffith still didn't look like a happy man.

"All right, Jenkins," Bartock said, "show everyone to their rooms."

"Do we get to pick our rooms?" Griffith asked.

Bartock gave the man a disinterested look and said, "Your rooms have already been assigned to you. When you come back down, there will be someone out in the foyer to direct you." He turned to his man and said, "All right, Jenkins."

"This way please, gentlemen and Miss Harrison," Jenkins said.

They started to file out of the room, setting down their cups and plates.

"Oh, one more thing," Bartock said. "I almost forgot this."

"What's that?" Easter asked.

"There will be no weapons allowed at the poker table or in the room during the game."

"Now wait—" Griffith started.

"Do you think you'll have need of a weapon, Mr. Griffith?" Bartock asked.

"I don't think I have to tell you, Bartock," Griffith said, "that I'm wanted in some states."

"Not this one, Mr. Griffith," Bartock said. "I checked. There won't be any need for weapons. I'll have enough security around the house and in the room. That's all. See you all later."

Bartock turned, effectively dismissing all of them.

TWENTY-THREE

Jenkins showed the guests to their rooms. First Griffith, then Easter, then Mason, and finally Paula Harrison and Clint. Their rooms were on the opposite side of the hall from the other three and next to each other.

"See you in a little while," Paula said to Clint as she entered her room.

Jenkins walked Clint down to his door and said, "This is yours."

"Are they all the same?" Clint asked.

"Virtually," Jenkins said. "Miss Harrison's is probably the nicest."

"Well, that's as it should be," Clint said.

"But they are all nice rooms," Jenkins said. "You should all be well rested for the next round."

"Thank you, Jenkins," Clint said.

Jenkins executed a small bow and said, "Someone will be up to ask if you would like water for a bath."

"Good," Clint said. "Thanks."

Clint entered his room and looked around. It was a nice-size room, with a four poster bed and a big porcelain bathtub. There was also an over-stuffed chair that he found extremely comfortable when he tried it. The entire room was comfortable, and he couldn't imagine what Paula's looked like if it was supposed to be nicer than this.

He had his shirt and boots off when there was a knock on his door. He opened it to find a young man standing out in the hall.

"Water?" the man asked.

"Yes, please."

"It will be right up," the man said.

"Has anyone else asked for it?"

"Yes, sir," the man said. "Mr. Mason and Miss Harrison."

"Do you have to carry it all yourself?"

"Oh no, sir," he said, "I have help. Don't worry. You won't have to wait long."

The young man was right. Before Clint knew it, there was another knock on the door. When he opened it, three young men walked in, each carrying two buckets. They made it to the tub without so much as a drop touching the floor. They made one more trip, and then Clint tipped them four bits each.

"Thank you very much," he said, closing the door after them.

He was naked and just about to step into the tub when there was another knock on his door. He cursed and considered not answering it, then grabbed a towel and wrapped it around his waist. When he opened the door he expected to find one of the young men, or Jenkins, but he certainly did not expect to find Paula Harrison—and especially not wearing just a towel.

"Let me in, quickly," she said, looking down the hall.

He backed up and allowed her to enter. She closed the door behind her, and then they both stood there in their towels.

"What—" he said, but she cut him off by allowing her towel to drop to the floor.

"I thought we'd better get this out of the way before the game started," she said.

"Wha—" he started again, but this time she cut him off by grabbing *his* towel and pulling it away from him.

"That is," she went on, "unless I was reading the signs wrong, and you're not interested."

He took in her body. She had high, firm breasts with brown nipples and wide hips. She was a big woman, with long, solid legs and thighs.

"No," she said, looking down, "I can see I wasn't wrong. You *are* interested, aren't you?"

TWENTY-FOUR

He was interested, there could be no doubt.

"I hope I'm not being too aggressive for you?" she said, moving closer, then taking him in her hand. "Ooh, it's so hot."

"Aggressive?" he said. "Is this aggressive?"

"No," she said. She slid one hand beneath him and cupped his genitals. "But this is."

He ran his hands over her back, down to her buttocks, which were big and solid, the way he liked a woman to be. He clutched her buttocks, and she moaned. She released her hold on his penis and balls and ran her hands up over his belly and chest until they were entwined behind his neck. She pulled his head down to her, and they kissed, avidly, mouths open and tongues anxious.

Abruptly Clint broke the kiss and lifted her in his arms. He carried her to the bed while she ran her lips over his neck. He lowered her to the bed, and she kept her hands locked around his neck, forcing his face against hers again. She moaned as they kissed, and he ran his hands over her body.

His left hand went down over her belly, through her pubic hair until he was probing her, finding her wet and ready. He slid one finger into her, and her hips jerked.

He climbed onto the bed with her, slid another finger into her, and found her clitoris with his thumb. This time she jerked and groaned into his mouth, then pulled her mouth away.

"Oh, God," she said as he moved his mouth down over her neck to the slopes of her breasts, and then to her nipples. He teased her, licking wet circles around her nipples with his tongue before closing his lips over one and sucking it.

"Ooh, yes, yes," she said, pulling his head close and lifting her hips. "Oh, please, now, Clint, now . . . ooh, you're making me so hot . . . I actually *ache*. . . ."

He slipped his hand from her, straddled her, and used his penis to rub up against her moist clitoris.

"Oh, God . . ." she said, and shuddered in orgasm. "Ooh, how'd you *do* that . . ."

He rubbed against her a few more times, teasing her, and then pushed the head of his penis until it slid inside of her. She gasped and lifted her ass off the bed, and he continued to enter her inch by inch until finally he was fully inside of her.

"Ohhh, yes, right there, that's where I want you," she said. She slid her heels up onto his buttocks, then closed her legs around him so that he could feel the strength in her thighs. He couldn't have gotten away from her now if he tried . . . and he had no intention of trying. . . .

• • •

They got into the bathtub together after that and washed each other. They were careful not to get water on the floor.

"You know," she said, sliding her foot between his legs, "if we made love in here we *would* get water all over the place."

"That wouldn't please our host," he said, reaching between his legs to grasp her foot in one hand.

"Maybe not," she said, "but I bet it would please us."

"And then everyone at the table would know about it," he said. "That would affect the game."

"It would, wouldn't it?" she said thoughtfully. "In fact, it would work to our advantage."

"How's that?"

She smiled and ran her foot along his thigh.

"Every time they looked at us they'd imagine us together, and they wouldn't be able to concentrate on their cards."

"Oh no," he said, "I know what you're thinking, and I'm against it."

"I know," she said. "So am I. We'll keep this as our little secret."

"Right."

"Speaking of secrets," she said. "Do you have any idea who this surprise player is?"

"None," he said. "Speaking of surprises, I'm still trying to get over *this* one."

"Why is it a surprise?" she asked. "I was attracted to you as soon as I saw you, and I know you were attracted to me."

"We all were."

"Maybe," she said, "but I had my eye on you. Once the game starts, we'll both be concentrating on that, and not on each other. This was the only chance we'd have to enjoy each other freely."

"There was always . . . after."

A slow smile spread over her lovely face and she said, "All right, then it was our *earliest* chance."

He couldn't remember the last time he had seen anything so lovely as she looked at that moment, all wet and gleaming.

TWENTY-FIVE

Clint got dressed first, then opened his door, stepped outside, and made sure the coast was clear so that Paula could slip back to her own room. Teasing him, she stepped into the hallway totally naked this time and walked slowly to her door, swaying her hips.

"Hurry up!" he whispered.

She turned when she reached the door, smiled at him, and struck a pose, one hand high up on the wall. The pose lifted her beautiful breasts, and she placed her other hand on her cocked hip.

"Paula—" he warned.

"Oh, okay," she said. "Chicken."

She opened her door and stepped inside, then peeked out once more to see if he was still watching. She blew him a kiss and ducked back in.

Down the hall he heard another door opening, and he stepped back into his room quickly and shut the door.

• • •

When Clint came downstairs at 10:45 there were three men standing in the foyer. They were all armed, wearing guns on their hips in fancy leather rigs.

"Sir?" one of them said.

"I'm Clint Adams."

Another man stepped forward and said, "Follow me, Mr. Adams."

Clint figured that each man had been assigned to one player in particular. Since there were only three left, that meant that at least two players were already in the room.

He followed the man to a large room dominated by a big round table right in the center. Griffith, Easter, and Cort Mason were seated at the table with Harry Bartock. In the center of the table were stacks of chips and several sealed decks of cards. There were eight chairs around the table, but only seven players. Clint couldn't remember if he knew or was assuming that Jenkins would deal.

The only player left upstairs was Paula, as far as Clint knew, and yet there were *two* men left in the foyer. That could only mean one thing.

The mysterious sixth player had arrived and was also upstairs.

"Ah, Clint," Harry Bartock said. "Tell Jenkins what you'd like to drink."

Jenkins was off to the side, behind a small bar. The security man who had led Clint to the room left.

"Nothing for me," Clint said. "I don't drink when I'm playing."

"Precisely what Mr. Mason said."

"Can't handle it, huh?" Griffith said.

Clint ignored him.

"I play better drunk," he said and downed the whiskey he was holding. "Jenkins, give me another!"

Clint saw Jenkins's shoulders stiffen, but he walked over, put a fresh glass of whiskey next to Griffith, and took away the empty glass.

Easter also had a glass of whiskey next to him, but apparently he wasn't as eager to finish it as his friend was.

"Have a seat, Clint," Bartock said. "The others will be here shortly."

"You mean Mr. Surprise finally got here?" Griffith asked.

Bartock looked at him and said with patience, "Yes, Mr. Griffith, we are all in the house now. In a few moments, we will all be here and ready to play."

"About time," Griffith mumbled.

The next player to arrive was Paula. She was wearing a gown similar to the one she had worn to dinner, but while the other had been green, this one was blue—and this one showed much more cleavage.

"Gentlemen."

Bartock, Clint, and Mason rose, and Bartock held her chair for her.

"I see we're all here but one," she said, looking around the table.

"Soon," Bartock said. "Would you like a drink?"

"Just a sherry," she said. "I'll have one just before we start."

Griffith and Easter were sitting next to each other. In fact, they were all seated at the poker table the same way they had been seated at dinner. Clint was to Bartock's right, one chair removed, which he assumed would be filled by the dealer, Jenkins. Paula sat to Bartock's left, Mason next to Paula, then Easter and then Griffith. When the last player arrived he'd be sitting between Griffith and Clint, to Clint's right.

Clint was able to see the door from where he was seated. He wondered if that had been deliberate on the part of his host.

Because he could see the door, Clint was the first to see the sixth player as he approached the room. He recognized the man with some surprise, but certainly no shock.

"Ah, our last player has arrived," Harry Bartock said, getting to his feet.

Griffith and Easter obviously didn't recognize the man. If Cort Mason did, he hid it well. Paula Harrison *did* recognize him, and it was clear that she *was* shocked to see him.

"For those of you who don't know who this gentleman is," Bartock said, "allow me to introduce you to . . . Mr. Ben Thompson."

TWENTY-SIX

"Wait a minute!" Jim Griffith shouted, standing up. "What kind of a setup is this?"

"Setup?" Harry Bartock said. "What do you mean?"

"You already said that Thompson recommended the woman for the game," Griffith said. "Now you expect us to play against both of them?"

"It just so happens," Bartock said, "Mr. Thompson refused my initial invitation and recommended Miss Harrison. He then discovered that he *would* be able to come and contacted me. I told him that he should come by all means. *I* told him there would be no problem."

"No problem, huh?"

"Ben," Paula Harrison said. "What a surprise."

Thompson came into the room and surveyed the people at the table.

"If anyone objects," he said, "I'll leave." He looked at Clint and said, "Hello, Adams. I didn't know you'd be here."

"I can say the same, Ben," Clint said. "Hello." Clint looked at Bartock and said, "Just for the record, I don't have any objection to Ben's playing."

"Neither do I," Cort Mason said. "All it does is raise the level of competition, and that's just fine with me."

Bartock looked at Tim Easter and said, "Mr. Easter?"

Easter swallowed and looked at Griffith, who was still standing. Griffith said nothing, so Easter had to make his own decision.

"I don't object," he said finally because he really wanted to play—and he didn't know when he'd ever get the chance to play in the same game as Cort Mason, Ben Thompson, and Clint Adams again.

Griffith glared at him, but he looked away.

"Mr. Griffith," Bartock said. "It appears yours is the only objection. If you choose to leave, we'll all understand."

Griffith looked around the table as everyone waited for him to reply.

"Sure," he said, "you'd all like me to leave, wouldn't you? Then you wouldn't have to deal with me at the table." He sat down and said, "Sorry, I'm staying."

"I have a request," Thompson said.

"Of course," Bartock said.

"May we question the seating arrangements?"

Bartock looked surprised.

"You have an objection?"

"Yes," Thompson said, "I don't want to sit next to Adams."

"Any particular reason?" Clint asked.

Thompson looked at Clint and said, "I'd like to sit where I can see both you and Mason."

"I have no objection to a change of seats," Bartock said. "Where would you like to sit?"

Thompson pointed at the seat presently occupied by Tim Easter. "There."

Bartock looked at Easter and said, "Do you object, Mr. Easter?"

"Well . . ." Easter said, but then he looked at Thompson and simply shook his head and stood up.

Once they were all seated, Bartock said, "Would you like a drink, Mr. Thompson?"

"A whiskey."

"Jenkins," Bartock said, "a whiskey for Mr. Thompson, and then you may come and begin dealing."

Jenkins brought Thompson his drink and then took his seat between Clint and Bartock.

"Does anyone object to Jenkins dealing?" Bartock asked.

No one did, although Griffith looked like he *wanted* to object.

"Very well. Jenkins will deal cards on the table faceup until an ace shows. That person will figuratively be the first dealer, and we will play dealer's choice. He will choose the game, and Jenkins will deal, and we will continue around the table in that manner. We do not play any wild card games, and we prefer to stick to the, uh, true poker games. Outlandish variations are not welcome. Any objections?"

There were none.

"Very well," Bartock said, "we will buy our chips, and the game will begin."

They each bought five hundred dollars in chips. The minimum bet to open would be ten dollars to start. As the game progressed, the stakes would no doubt increase, but now they would start moderately. When a player was tapped out, he would be able to purchase more chips for as long as he—or she—wished to continue playing.

Once they had their chips, Jenkins dealt each player one card faceup on the table in front of them until the first ace showed. It dropped on the second go-round in front of Paula Harrison.

"Ah," Bartock said with a gracious smile, "and we begin with the lady. What is your game, Miss Harrison?"

"Seven-card stud," she said, and the game proceeded.

TWENTY-SEVEN

Things went well right from the start for Thompson and Paula Harrison, which fueled Griffith's anger at having to play in the same game with them. The more he lost, and the more they won, the angrier he got, and the more reckless he got, the more he lost.

Clint was watching Thompson and Paula the first hour and could detect no collusion between them—but then, he hadn't expected to. He knew Thompson's reputation as a gambler was an honest one—at least, as honest as a gambler could be.

Griffith, Easter, and Bartock did most of the losing the first few hours, but Bartock took it a lot better than the other two did. While Thompson and Paula did most of the winning, Mason and Clint held their own and were just about even after four hours of play.

"I call for a break," Griffith said, running his hands through his hair.

"Fine," Bartock said.

"And a new deck of cards when we come back," Mason said.

"I'll see to it," Jenkins said.

"You may all help yourselves to refreshments," Bartock said, standing up. "I am going to go and freshen up a bit."

Bartock left the room while Griffith and Easter went to the bar. Jenkins remained in the room but stood away from the players.

"I'm going to freshen up, too," Paula said. "Excuse me."

"I'm just going to step outside for a breath of fresh air, and a cigar," Mason said.

That left Clint and Ben Thompson sitting at the table alone.

"Been a long time, Adams."

"How've you been, Ben?"

"Not bad," the other man said.

"Never thought I'd see you in a game that called for no guns."

"I could say the same thing about you, Clint," Thompson said. He looked over at the two armed men who were standing at the doorway and added, "I don't think we'll be needing them at this game, though, do you?"

"That depends," Clint said, looking over at Griffith and Easter, who were deep in conversation.

"Oh, I don't think we'll have any real trouble out of those two," Thompson said.

"What about the woman, Ben?" Clint asked.

"What about her?"

"She's pretty good," Clint said. "She says she worked with you. Did you teach her?"

"Not really," Thompson said. "I worked with her a bit on her temperament. She used to be real impatient. Her card sense has always been sound, though."

"Well, whatever you did, it worked," Clint said. "She's good."

"What do you think of Mason?" Thompson asked.

"Sound," Clint said. "He doesn't take many chances. I think that by grinding it out he'll probably come out ahead more often than not."

Thompson nodded his agreement.

"And our host?"

Clint hesitated and then said, "I think he just likes to play for a lot of money with high-priced talent. He doesn't fit in, though, as a player."

"Ever play here before?"

"No," Clint said. "Been invited a few times, but I was never able to make it before."

"Same with me," Thompson said. "I was supposed to be at a game right now in San Francisco, but that one fell through, so I decided to come here."

"Well," Clint said, "glad to have you here, Ben. Livens the game up a bit."

Clint saw Griffith and Easter returning to the table. He looked at Thompson and said, "Buy you a drink?"

"What?" Thompson said, and then he saw the other two men returning. "Oh, sure, why not?"

He and Clint stood up and went around one side of the table while Griffith and Easter went around the other.

Clint poured himself a small whiskey and a larger one for Thompson.

"Trying to get me drunk?" Thompson asked.

"I just don't like drinking while I'm playing."

"Well," Thompson said, accepting the whiskey, "I like drinking anytime."

Cort Mason was the first of the players to return. He joined Clint and Thompson at the bar. Clint poured him a whiskey and handed it to him. They made small talk about gamblers they all knew until Paula Harrison came back. Instead of going to the table, she walked over to join them. She was wearing the same gown, but the smell of her perfume was more intense.

"A drink?" Clint asked.

"A small one," Paula said.

He held it out to her, and she made sure that her fingers brushed the back of his hand before she took it from him. He wanted to scratch his hand, but resisted the urge.

"Is he antisocial?" Paula asked, indicating Jenkins, who was still standing in a corner by himself.

"He's the dealer," Thompson said. "He's just maintaining a discreet distance."

"Maybe you should go over and *ask* him if he's antisocial," Mason said to Paula.

"I don't think so," she said, giving Mason a cold look.

"Hey," Mason said, "I only meant—"

"I know what you meant, Mr. Mason," Paula said. "In this room I'm not a woman, I'm just another poker player. I'll thank you to remember that."

She put her glass down and walked back to the table while the three men watched appreciatively.

"Not in that dress she's not," Mason said.

TWENTY-EIGHT

At four in the morning Bartock suggested suspending the game until they all got some sleep, since it was the first night and some of them had traveled that day.

"Hey, what about me?" Griffith demanded. "I'm just startin' to win."

Easter was still losing, so when they put it to a vote everyone voted to break except Griffith, who stormed angrily from the room muttering something about a conspiracy.

It went against the grain for Clint to leave his money on the table, but it was a house rule so he went along with it.

"I know how you feel," Thompson said as they walked to the stairs. "It doesn't sit right with me, either."

"Don't worry," Bartock said from behind them. "Your money will be there tomorrow. I personally guarantee it."

Thompson turned, looked at Bartock, and said, "You bet you will."

Bartock was taken aback for just a moment and then forced a smile onto his face.

"Believe me, gentlemen," he said, speaking specifically to Clint and Ben Thompson, "I would never invite two such famed gentlemen as yourselves here for a game and then try to steal from you. I doubt that would be very healthy for me."

"You're right about that, too," Clint said. "Good night, Mr. Bartock."

"Yes, of course," Bartock said, "good night, gentlemen. I have, uh, some work to do in my office. I will see you in the morning, for breakfast. Remember, breakfast will be from nine a.m. to ten a.m."

"I'll be there," Clint said.

Cort Mason had already walked upstairs with Paula Harrison, and Jenkins had disappeared somewhere, so Clint and Thompson went up the steps together now.

Bartock watched them go, and when they were out of sight, he rubbed his palms together gleefully, said, "Marvelous," and then turned to the two guards on the door.

"Remember, gentlemen," he told them, "if so much as one chip is missing, I will hold you both personally responsible."

"Nobody's gettin' into that room, sir," one of them said.

"That's very good," Bartock said, pointing to the steps, "because those two gentlemen would be very upset, and you do know who they are, don't you?"

The guards exchanged nervous glances, and one of them said, "We know, sir."

"Good," Bartock said, "very good. Oh, this is excellent!"

He turned and hurried down the hall to his office.

Thompson's room turned out to be on the other side of Paula Harrison's.

"Good night, Clint," he said at his door.

Clint kept walking and said over his shoulder, "Night, Ben."

He entered his room, unbuttoning his shirt. There was a gas lamp on the wall next to the door, and he reached to turn it up. As the glow got brighter and lit the room, he saw that he was not alone—but then he wasn't entirely surprised by this.

"You're not too sleepy, are you?" a naked Paula Harrison asked from his bed.

"I don't think so," he said. Then he looked down at himself and added, "No, apparently not."

"Good," she said. She rolled over onto her back, her breasts flattening slightly. She raised one leg and ran her hand along it. "Poker excites me, and there's only one thing that relaxes me enough to sleep afterward."

Clint kicked off his boots and peeled off his pants as fast as he could. At that moment he was anything but sleepy.

In his room Jim Griffith was seething. There was an obvious plot going on to keep him from winning, and it was because he was the only one with nerve enough to speak up when something was bothering him. Even Tim Easter was going against him. Well, they were going to see a new Griffith at the poker table tomorrow. Yep, tomorrow was going to be his day.

Tim Easter entered his room, sat on the bed fully clothed, and wondered what the hell he was doing there. He knew he'd been invited only because they needed another body. He also knew that he was hopelessly outclassed here in more ways than one—and now Griffith was mad at him, and he sure didn't need *that*.

He was already down half his buy-in. Maybe it was just time to cut and run.

In his room Cort Mason started to undress, then stopped and briefly considered walking across the hall to Paula Harrison's room and knocking on the door. He wouldn't have to say anything when she answered. What other possible reason could he have for knocking at this hour? But . . . perhaps it was too soon in the game for that. Besides, he really *did* need to get some rest before the game resumed tomorrow.

He undressed the rest of the way and went to bed thinking about the inside straight he'd tried to fill during the second hour of the game. It was *certainly* too early in the game to have tried that!

Ben Thompson did not undress immediately. He walked to the window and looked out, seeing

that his room overlooked the front of the house.
There was no light outside, and it was almost a
moonless night. He loosened his tie, took it off,
and undid the top button of his shirt.

His room was identical to Clint Adams's, with
the same armchair. He walked over to it, sat
down, and slowly removed his boots. He hadn't
expected Clint Adams to be here. The pickings,
with Adams in the game, would not be easy.
Griffith and Easter posed no threat, and neither
did Bartock, the host. Cort Mason had a rep, but
it appeared to be overblown. That meant he only
had to worry about Paula and Adams. Paula he
thought he could handle. He didn't think it was
time for the student to conquer the master.

That left Clint Adams, a man he respected but
admittedly had never quite become comfortable
around. They had friends in common, notably Bat
Masterson and Luke Short. They had both known
Bill Hickok, but Adams and Hickok had been very
close friends, and Thompson and Hickok had never liked each other.

Too much thinking, he told himself. With
Adams in the game, it was bound to be interesting. And who knew? Maybe they'd start to think
differently of each other on a personal level. A
lot of Ben Thompson's friends were dead. Lately,
he'd been thinking it might be time to make some
new ones.

Jenkins, who had gone to his room immediately after the game, returned sometime later and
confronted the guards.

"Has anyone come back down?" he asked.

"No, sir."

"That's good," Jenkins said. "I'm going inside now for a while."

"Yes, sir."

He opened the double doors that led to the room, passed between the two guards, and closed the doors behind him.

TWENTY-NINE

Paula did not go back to her room that night. Clint let her stay only once she promised that they would get some sleep and be up for breakfast.

He opened his eyes later and felt her between his legs. He looked down at the top of her head and reached for her just as she took him fully into her mouth.

"Jesus," he said, lifting his butt off the bed as she began to suck on him. She did not leave him alone until she had drained him completely. Then she gazed up at him with a satisfied look on her face and said, "See? I told you we'd be up for breakfast."

Clint went down to breakfast first because it wouldn't look right if they went together, and because it would take Paula longer to get ready anyway. It was close to nine, and Bartock was the only one there. Clint wondered if *he* would be there if Paula hadn't awakened him.

"Good morning," Clint said.

120

Bartock looked up at him and smiled.

"Ah, I had a bet with myself as to who the first one down would be."

"And?" Clint asked.

"I won," Bartock said happily. "Please, sit."

"How will the cook know I'm here?" Clint asked.

"Cook!" Bartock shouted. He smiled at Clint and said, "Now she knows."

Clint couldn't get over how incredibly rested Bartock looked—and how young. It was as if he was so happy that they were all there, and that he was playing poker with them, that he was looking even younger than he was.

Maybe that was it. Maybe this was his fountain of youth.

The cook came out with more scrambled eggs, rashers of bacon, and fresh biscuits. She asked Clint if he wanted some flapjacks.

"Sure," Clint said. "Why not?"

She was a large woman in her fifties with huge fleshy arms and a quick smile.

"I hear you've eaten at Red's," she said.

"That's right, I have."

"Well," she said, shaking her head, "Lord knows Red's been outcookin' me since she came to town, but I'll do my best." She leaned over and said, "I wouldn't even have a job here if she'd agreed to work for Mr. Bartock."

"Now, now, Martha," Bartock said, "there's nothing wrong with being the second-best cook in the county."

"I guess not," Martha said. She laughed and said

to Clint, "Leastways, I'm the best paid. I'll have those flapjacks in here in a jiff."

"She's a dear woman," Bartock said, "but she's right. If I could get Red to cook for me, I'd fire Martha in a minute."

"Must be nice for Martha to have such job security," Clint said.

"I hire the best available to me, Clint," Bartock said. "When Red turned me down, Martha was the best available to me, but she knows she wasn't my first choice. I think it's important for people to know exactly where they stand, don't you?"

"Of course," Clint said, wondering if his host was trying to tell him something.

"Let me ask you something," Bartock said. "I realize now what a mistake I made extending invitations to the game to Mr. Easter and Mr. Griffith."

"I was wondering about that myself," Clint said. "They don't seem to fit in with the theme of your game. I mean, in the past I've heard that you had some pretty heavy talent playing."

"Oh yes," Bartock said. "One year I had Bat Masterson *and* Wyatt Earp *and* Luke Short at the same table."

Clint had played poker with all of those gentlemen at the same table a few times but didn't mention it. Bartock seemed so pleased to have gotten them together.

"This year it just seemed that most of the people I wanted had other things to do," Bartock said. "I asked around and was given the names of Griffith and Easter, but now I'm sorry I invited them."

"Well," Clint said, "from what I've seen, they won't last very long anyway."

"That is what I'm hoping," Bartock said, "but let me ask you, since you are experienced with men of this . . . nature. Should I expect trouble from them—especially Mr. Griffith—when they do lose?"

Clint thought a moment and then said, "I wouldn't worry about Easter. I get the feeling he might pull out even before he loses."

"And Mr. Griffith?"

"Well, that's going to depend on a lot of things."

"Like what?"

"Well, like how badly he loses," Clint said. "Some men don't mind losing, but when they lose badly they don't react well."

"I see," Bartock said. "Would you suggest increasing security?"

"Will you always have two men on the door?" Clint asked.

"Yes, that's my plan."

Clint shrugged and said, "Then I think that should be enough. It might even be all you need to keep him from starting trouble."

"I see," Bartock said. "Well, thank you for your advice. I appreciate it."

"Sure."

Martha entered with the flapjacks just as Ben Thompson arrived, and then the other players began to arrive one by one. The last to arrive was—of course—Paula Harrison, who also surprised Clint by looking remarkably well rested. She had obviously been telling the truth. Sex made her sleep like a baby. She smiled at everyone, bid them good morning, and sat at Harry Bartock's right hand.

Clint noticed that Tim Easter was looking particularly uncomfortable this morning. It was his guess that the man had realized, either last night at the table or after he'd gone to his room, that he was hopelessly outclassed.

What surprised Clint was that Jim Griffith looked relaxed and well rested, and was smiling and talking freely with Cort Mason, who was seated next to him. Considering the mood the man had been in the night before, during the game and after, this new mood of his was something that surprised Clint and made him curious.

"I haven't seen your man Jenkins, this morning," Clint said.

"Jenkins is probably still asleep, poor man," Bartock said. "When he's dealing in these annual games, I usually allow some leeway in his other duties. He'll be up and around in due time."

"What time will we start the game up again?" Griffith asked.

"Eager, are we, Mr. Griffith?"

Griffith smiled at his host and said, "I do have a ways to come back, don't I, Mr. Bartock?"

"I detect an attitude change in you, Mr. Griffith," Bartock said. "You are not as . . . irritable as you were yesterday."

Griffith smiled again at Bartock and said, "Sleep does wonders for a man's attitude, Mr. Bartock."

"Yes, well," Bartock said, "it *is* a distinct improvement."

"I think you'll find," Griffith said, "that the same will be true of my poker playing."

"Well," Bartock said, "in that case, I guess the sooner we start the better. We'll begin as soon as Jenkins appears—which, I assure all of you, will be very shortly. Even when he sleeps late he's up earlier than most—ah, see what I mean?"

Jenkins entered the room and stared at the players and his employer.

"We were just talking about you, Jenkins."

"Yes, sir," Jenkins said. "I'm sorry I was, uh, tardy this morning."

"We'll be starting the game right after breakfast, Jenkins," Bartock said. "Go into the kitchen and get yourself something to eat."

"Yes, sir," Jenkins said. "I'll be ready, sir."

"I know you will," Bartock said as Jenkins walked around the table and went into the kitchen.

"He's invaluable to me," Bartock said as the door swung shut behind his man, "just invaluable."

THIRTY

The game started up promptly after breakfast, and, true to his word, Jim Griffith was a different man. He didn't complain about a thing, and he started winning. It was clear to Clint, and the others, that when the man had his temper under control, he was a much better poker player.

Easter, on the other hand, began to lose even more and faster than he had the night before. He had no confidence, and even when he got good cards, he misplayed them. It was clear that he would not last very much longer in the game.

True to everyone's expectations, it was about three in the afternoon when Tim Easter came to the end of his rope. Sweating profusely, his hands shaking, he tossed in the last of his chips and stood up.

"I think, uh, I mean, I guess that's it for me," he stammered.

"Leaving already, Mr. Easter?" Bartock asked. "You can buy more chips, you know."

"No thanks," Easter said. "I've already bought back in once."

"Oh, that's right, you did, didn't you?" Bartock said. "Well, if you feel you *must* leave . . ."

"Yeah," Easter said, "yeah, I don't think I— I mean, I think I should. I just can't . . . you know . . ."

"Yeah, Tim," Griffith said, "we know. Listen, it was good seein' you again, but if you're gonna go, then go so we can get on with it."

Easter cast a hurt look Griffith's way. Maybe he expected more sympathy from the man who was supposed to be his friend.

"Yeah, okay," Easter said.

"Mr. Easter," Bartock said, "you may go up-stairs and freshen up, but I'm afraid that if you are out of the game, I cannot offer you the hospitality of my house anymore. You understand, of course."

"Sure," Easter said, "sure, Mr. Bartock. Uh, thanks for the invitation to play."

Bartock waved his hand at Easter and said to Jenkins, "You can deal, Jenkins."

Easter left the room as Jenkins started dealing another hand of seven-card stud. . . .

By dinnertime Clint had started to win a little, rather than holding his own, as he had been doing since the night before. The big winners during this second session had been Jim Griffith and, to a lesser extent, Cort Mason. The luck Ben Thompson and Paula Harrison had been enjoy-ing the night before had not quite deserted them, but they were not dominating the winning on this day.

The only player who was not enjoying *some* sort of reversal of luck was their host, Harry Bartock. He had been losing the night before, and he continued to lose as they approached a dinner break.

In fact, it was Bartock himself who called the game to a halt so that they *could* eat dinner.

They all stood up and stretched, trying to work the kinks out of their bodies from the longer session.

"Anyone for a before-dinner drink?" Bartock asked.

"Sure," Clint said. Ben Thompson also accepted. Griffith, Mason, and Paula Harrison said they were going up to their rooms to freshen up before dinner. Clint did not miss the meaningful glance Paula gave him as she left the room. He wondered if anyone else had picked up on it as well.

"That was a hard day's work, gentlemen," Bartock said, pouring them each a sherry. "Especially when you're losing the way I am."

"The cards are cruel sometimes," Thompson said, accepting his glass.

"Your luck will change," Clint added.

"Ah," Bartock said with a sad smile, "I think we all know that is not the case. By now you gentlemen have tumbled onto my little secret."

"Secret?" Clint asked.

"Which secret is that?" Ben Thompson asked.

"Come, come, gentlemen," Bartock said. "By

now you've discovered what an abysmal poker player I am."

"Well . . ." Thompson said.

"Why do you do it, then?" Clint asked. "I mean, if you're so bad and you know it."

Bartock sipped his drink thoughtfully.

"I enjoy it," he said. "I especially like the company. Face it, where else would I get to sit in the same room with Clint Adams and Ben Thompson?"

"You could travel," Clint said. "You'd find some enjoyment in that, and you'd meet a lot of people."

"Perhaps," Bartock said, "perhaps you're right, but I'm not ready to give up on my little game . . . not just yet anyway."

"Well," Thompson said, "you do seem to have the money to lose, don't you?"

"Oh my, yes," Bartock said. "It would take more than one of these poker games to break me."

"Glad to hear it," Clint said. "I wish I could say the same."

"Clint," Bartock said, "I don't think you ever have to worry about going broke in a poker game, do you?"

Clint looked at Thompson, who simply shrugged.

"It's happened once or twice, Mr. Bartock," Clint said.

"Oh, please," Bartock said, "both of you must start calling me Harry."

"Is that in private?" Clint asked. "Or at any time?"

"At this stage of the game?" Bartock said. "I think we should all be on a first-name basis, don't you?"

Thompson looked at Clint and said, "I always like to call a man by his first name when I'm taking money from him, don't you?"

"Oh, sure," Clint said, "the friendlier the better."

"Speaking of friendlier," Bartock said, "what do you gentlemen think of the change that seems to have come over our Mr. Griffith?"

"I think," Clint said, "that he went to his room last night, did some heavy thinking, and came down this morning knowing what he had to do."

"I agree," Thompson said. "The man sure is a better poker player than I thought, but I'd say only when he has his temper in check."

"Well," Bartock said, "after dinner, maybe we should see if we can get him riled up a bit, maybe lose his concentration?"

Clint and Thompson exchanged glances that indicated they didn't think that was such a good idea.

"Oh, gentlemen, gentlemen," Harry Bartock said, slapping them both on the back, "I'm kidding, just kidding. Come on, let's all freshen up before dinner. We have a lot of poker playing ahead of us."

THIRTY-ONE

When Clint got up to his room he found Paula Harrison there, and she was frantic.

"Where have you been?" she demanded.

Actually, being frantic and nearly angry—*and* naked—she presented a pretty comical picture at that moment, and he couldn't help but start to laugh.

"What's so funny?" she demanded. She got to her knees on the bed and planted her fists on her hips.

"You are," he said. "You look ridiculous, naked and all upset. What are you upset about?"

"I've been *waiting* for you!" she said. "What took you so long? We have to go down for dinner soon, and we don't have much time."

Clint frowned and said, "Wait a second, here. Do you expect me to come running up here to . . . to . . . service you every time we take a break from the game?"

She compressed her lips for a moment and sat down on the bed and stared at him.

"All right," she said, "confession time."

"Go ahead," he said, "I'm listening."

"Poker," she said, "and sex are . . . connected for me."

"What?"

"I know, I know," she said, "it sounds silly, but I've always found that I play better when I'm . . . when I've been satisfied."

Clint frowned, thinking, and then said, "Now . . . let me get this straight in my mind, okay? You play better poker when you've had sex?"

"Right."

"Just before the game?"

"Well . . . a little before, yeah," she said. "So, now that you understand, come to bed. Maybe we have time before dinner—"

"Wait, wait, wait," he said, waving his hands, "hold on. You're telling me that by having sex with you, I'm helping you beat me in poker?"

Paula hesitated, then said, "Well, yes . . . if you want to look at it that way."

"What other way is there to look at it?" he asked.

"Clint . . . come on . . ."

"Paula," he said, "I think you'd better go to your room and get ready for dinner."

She looked at him, a shocked expression on her face.

"You—you're sending me away?"

"I came here to play poker, Paula," he said, "*and* win. Sex with you is nice—in fact, it's wonderful—but I've never paid for sex before, and I'm not going to start now—and that's what I'd be doing."

She stared at him and opened her mouth, but the words wouldn't come.

"I can't believe this," she finally managed to say.

"Believe it," he said. "I'm sorry—*believe* me, I'm sorry. . . ."

She got off the bed and hurriedly pulled her clothes on for the walk down the hall. She walked past him to the door, opened it, and then turned to face him.

"You realize that if I don't get what I need from you, I'll have to get it from someone else," she explained, "from some other man?"

"I know that," Clint said, "but at least then I'll know that if you beat me, *I* didn't help you."

She stared at him, then shook her head and left the room, closing the door gently behind her.

Clint went over and sat on the bed. The sheet was ripe with her scent. He shook his head at himself. He couldn't remember the last time he'd made a beautiful, naked woman leave his room.

The things he did to win at poker.

He wondered whom she would pick. Cort Mason? Their host, Bartock himself? And what about her old friend and mentor, Ben Thompson? Had they ever been together before? Would she pick him?

Jesus, he thought, why drive myself crazy even thinking about it?

He got up, poured some water into a basin, and started to wash for dinner.

THIRTY-TWO

Dinner was a bit strained for Clint. Paula alternated between not looking at him and looking at him boldly. Clint couldn't help but wonder which man she had chosen and found himself looking around the table, trying to figure it out.

Bartock was doing most of the talking, and a lot of it was directed to Paula. Everyone listened to their host politely, but Clint noticed Mason and Griffith talking quite a bit together. Try as he might, though, he couldn't detect anything going on between Paula and any one of the other men. Maybe she had only had time to pick one out before dinner. Maybe the lucky guy would go to his room that night after the game broke up and find Paula in *his* bed.

Lucky guy . . . lucky in love, unlucky at cards, right? Apparently, not Paula Harrison.

The game started up again after dinner, and it soon became obvious that this was the night the stakes were going to go higher.

During the second hour of the session, Jim Griffith, who was high on the table with a pair of kings, said, "Isn't it about time we raised the stakes?"

He looked around the table, and there were no dissenters.

"I bet a hundred," he said.

"Raise a hundred," Ben Thompson said, almost immediately.

Each player had three cards on the table, with two cards left to come in the game. Griffith obviously had kings, and maybe more. Thompson's cards on the table appeared to be mismatched. Two of them, however, were hearts. If he had two more hearts in the hole, then he was working on a flush. However, Clint doubted that Thompson would raise this early in this particular session on a four-card flush. The chances were more likely that he had a pair in the hole that matched one of the cards on the table, giving him three of a kind.

Clint had a four-card straight, but two of the cards he needed to fill in were already out, and with Griffith raising the limit and Thompson raising, it was obvious that they already had something, while he was still looking.

"Fold," he said.

"I call," Harry Bartock said.

One thing Clint had noticed about Bartock was that he rarely folded. As long as he had a distant prayer of making something, he stayed in the game. The first rule of poker for Clint Adams was: You can't win every hand. That meant that you couldn't possibly *play* every hand and hope to have a winning game.

"I fold," Paula Harrison said and looked across the table at Clint.

Paula had not taken a hand yet, and Clint was beginning to feel that—if what she had said was true—she *hadn't* had sex with anyone before dinner. If that was really why she was losing, she had to be blaming him.

As he watched, she began to study the men at the table. Was she picking out his potential replacement even then?

"I call," Cort Mason said.

"Cards coming," Jenkins said and dealt out the remaining players' sixth cards.

Griffith didn't improve, but he bet anyway, even though Thompson had raised. That was because Thompson had not noticeably improved either.

"Two hundred," he said.

"Raise two hundred," Thompson said.

"Tryin' to convince me that you have somethin', Ben?" Griffith asked.

"You'll have to pay to find out," Thompson said.

"I call," Bartock said, tossing four hundred dollars' worth of chips into the pot despite the fact that his cards were even more mismatched then Ben Thompson's.

Bartock had maybe a little over a thousand dollars in chips left on the table in front of him. If he didn't win this hand, he'd probably have to buy more chips before the next one.

"No," Mason said, "not me."

"Well," Griffith said, "now we get to it, don't we?" He was looking at Thompson.

"I guess so," Thompson said.

"Your two hundred," Griffith said, tossing chips, "and five hundred more."

Griffith's good day had continued after dinner, and he had quite a stack of chips in front of him. He pushed five hundred dollars' worth into the pot and sat staring at Thompson with a very satisfied look on his face.

Thompson sat studying Griffith for a few moments, then silently pushed the same amount of chips into the pot.

"Call."

Now all eyes turned to Bartock, the only player left in the game.

"I'll need to buy more chips now to stay in the hand," Bartock said. "Does anyone object?"

Jenkins, as the dealer, looked around the table and waited for answers.

"Hell, no," Griffith said, "the more money in the pot the better."

"Go ahead," Thompson said. "We'll wait."

"Thank you," Bartock said. "Jenkins, let me have another twenty-five hundred dollars."

"You better buy more than that," Griffith said, "or you'll just have to buy again after the hand."

"I will if I lose this hand, of course," Bartock said, staring boldly across the table at Jim Griffith.

Bartock collected his chips from Jenkins and then slid the appropriate amount into the pot.

"I call."

"Last card coming out," Jenkins said and dealt it out facedown.

The three remaining players—Griffith, Thompson, and Bartock—had all the cards they were going to get now. Jenkins put the deck down on the table, and Clint noticed that he was watching this hand with a lot more interest than he had shown so far.

"Your bet, Mr. Griffith," he said.

"Yeah, well," Griffith said, "five hundred."

"Call five hundred," Thompson said, "and raise five hundred."

"That's a thousand to you, sir," Jenkins said to Bartock.

"Yes, Jenkins," Bartock said. He counted out a thousand and pushed it into a pot, and then while everyone looked on incredulously, he counted out another two thousand and pushed *that* into the pot. That left him with no chips at all in front of him.

"Call and raise two thousand," he said.

"What?" Griffith said, staring.

Ben Thompson remained silent but narrowed his eyes to get a better look at the cards Bartock had on the table.

"Mr. Bartock," Griffith said, shaking his head, "I know you're our host, but if you keep playin' poker like this, somebody at this table is gonna end up ownin' this ranch."

"The bet is to you, Mr. Griffith," Bartock said.

Clint had to hold back a smile while he watched. He suspected now that Harry Bartock just might be a better poker player than he had been letting on the whole time. Although there was not an exorbitant amount of money in the pot, Clint did not think it was the money Bartock was playing for in this particular hand. He had simply chosen this hand to sandbag somebody, and Griffith and Thompson had ended up his victims.

Griffith couldn't believe that Bartock was serious, but he didn't have the balls right at that moment to raise so he simply said, "I'll call you, just to go easy on you."

He pushed two thousand dollars into the pot.

"Mr. Thompson?" Jenkins said.

Thompson had a resigned look on his face. He flicked a brief look at Clint, who knew that Thompson now *knew* what had happened, but there wasn't much he could do about it. Clint was convinced that Thompson had Griffith beat. That left only Bartock, and Thompson was going to *have* to call the bet.

"I call." Thompson pushed his chips into the pot.

"Let's see 'em, Bartock," Griffith said, almost in a growl.

"My, my," Bartock said, turning his cards over, "sometimes I almost believe in God."

His three hole cards were all fours, matching one that he had on the table.

"Four of a kind," Jenkins said. He looked at Griffith and Thompson and said, "Gentlemen?"

"Jesus," Griffith said, throwing his cards into the pot. They spread out across the table, but Clint could see that he had three kings.

He looked at Thompson, who simply pushed his cards into the center of the table facedown and said to Bartock, "It's yours."

"Why, thank you," Bartock said and reached for his chips.

At the same time Griffith reached for Ben Thompson's cards and said, "Well, what did you have?"

In one swift move Thompson brought his hand down on Griffith's hand, pinning it to the table. Pinned beneath the two hands were Ben Thompson's cards.

"Don't touch my cards," he said.

"I just wanna see if I beat you," Griffith said, his tone almost a whine.

"You paid to see his cards," Thompson said, indicating Bartock with a nod of his head, "not mine."

"Jeez, Thompson—"

"If you touch my cards again, Griffith," Thompson said to the other man, "I'll break your hand. When you've *paid* to see *my* cards, you can. Understand?"

Griffith stared at Thompson for a few moments, then looked around the table to find everyone looking at him.

"Well, sure, Ben," he said finally, his tone resigned, "sure, I understand."

Thompson removed his hand, and Griffith reclaimed his. Jenkins reached out and raked the cards in, gathering them to deal.

"I think," Cort Mason said, "that after that hand we need a new deck."

THIRTY-THREE

Jim Griffith's luck went south after that hand, and he started losing heavily. He was the one who had initiated the increase of the stakes, and now he was the one who was paying for it. The more he lost, the angrier he got, and the angrier he got, the more he lost.

Cort Mason also started to lose, almost as badly as Griffith. Griffith just wasn't getting any cards. In Mason's case, however, he was constantly losing with the second-best hand on the table.

At the close of the session, about four a.m., Griffith was almost tapped out. He had enough to begin the next day, but if he didn't start winning, he knew he'd be on his way out the door.

Mason, being the gambler that he was, had brought enough money to withstand a cold streak, but this wasn't really a cold streak. The cards were there, he was just losing with them. He knew that if he suddenly hit a *real* cold streak, he'd be out of the game in no time.

After winning that hand with four of a kind, Bartock started to do better, but Clint had revised his opinion once again. Perhaps the man wasn't as bad a player as he had originally thought, but neither was he as good as that one hand had made him look. More and more it looked as if he had just gotten lucky.

Paula Harrison was ahead at the end of that session, but she had lost most of her profits from the sessions before.

The two players who had suddenly started winning and had most of the money on the table between them were Ben Thompson and Clint Adams.

"I think we should call it a night," Bartock said after a particularly brutal hand in which he *and* Mason had lost with flushes to Clint's full house.

"You've got my vote," Mason said. "I've never been second-best so many times in my life."

Since the end of the session had been announced, Jim Griffith stood up and simply walked out without a word to anyone.

"At least I'm losing with decent cards," Mason said, standing up. "Griffith hasn't seen a decent hand since *he* raised the stakes."

"It happens like that sometimes," Ben Thompson said.

"Anyone for a drink?" Bartock asked.

"I'm going to bed, gentlemen," Paula Harrison said. "See you in the morning." She left the room without throwing that special glance Clint's way.

"I think I'll turn in, too," Cort Mason said. "Good night."

Bartock turned to Clint and Thompson and asked, "Can I interest you gentlemen in a nightcap?"

"Sure," Clint said, "why not?"

"I'll take one," Thompson said.

"Excellent."

Clint looked around, but Jenkins had mysteriously disappeared.

They walked to the bar where Bartock poured out three glasses of sherry.

"Actually, I'm glad the others have left," he said, handing Clint and Thompson their glasses. "I have something I'd like to show the two of you. The others wouldn't appreciate it."

"What is it?" Clint asked.

"Come with me."

Bartock led them to the far wall where a large painting was hanging. Bartock reached for the wall and Clint heard a click. Suddenly, the wall—painting and all—swung open.

"A hidden room?" Thompson asked.

"Not really a room," Bartock said, opening the "door" wider. "Take a look."

It was not large enough to be called a room, but there was about three feet of space behind the wall—and every inch was taken up by guns.

Clint looked at the collection appreciatively. Bartock seemed to have guns from the earliest pistols ever made—snaphaunces and flintlocks—up to the double-action Colts of the present day.

Most of them were hanging on the wall, but some of them were in glass cases. One in particular—a seventeenth-century snaphaunce—was in a glass case on a velvet base.

"Quite a collection," Ben Thompson said.

"Yes," Bartock said, "I'm very proud of it."

"Since you like collecting guns so much," Thompson asked, "do you know how to use one?"

"Oh my, no," Bartock said. "I'm a terrible shot. That's why I keep men around me who *can* use guns."

"Well," Thompson said, "seems a shame to keep all these weapons locked up."

"They're worth quite a lot of money," Bartock said.

"Who else knows about your collection?" Clint asked.

"Just the people who work for me," Bartock said. "Why?"

"It's not the kind of thing I'd spread around," Clint said.

"Oh," Bartock said, "I assure you, even if someone wanted to steal from me, they'd never get on the grounds, let alone in the house."

"I hope you're right," Clint said. He finished his sherry and took one last look at the assortment of weapons in Bartock's collection. "Impressive."

"Thank you," Bartock said. "I knew that the two of you would appreciate it, that's why I showed it to you."

He closed the wall, and Clint heard a lock click in.

"And now perhaps we should turn in," Bartock said. "Due to the lateness of the hour, I think I'll extend the breakfast hour tomorrow."

"That's very kind of you," Clint said.

"I also believe that tomorrow's session will probably, uh, pare us down a bit more, don't you?"

"Yes," Thompson said. "I think we'll probably empty another couple of seats tomorrow."

"Perhaps," Bartock said, "even mine."

"Good night," Clint said.

He and Thompson walked up the steps together.

"I doubt that he would ever quit the game before it was over," Thompson said.

"He's got the money to stay in, no matter how much he loses, that's for sure," Clint said, "but I don't think Griffith will last more than another hour or so."

"And Mason looks like he's ready to tap out," Thompson said. "Bartock will just be taking up a seat. That will leave you, and Paula, and me."

For a moment Clint thought about asking Thompson if he knew about Paula's particular formula for winning poker, but then he decided against it.

At Thompson's door, Clint said, "Yes, I guess it will get down to the three of us."

"When that happens," Thompson said, "let's jack the stakes up even higher. This place is starting to wear thin on me."

"You know," Clint said, "I'd kind of like to get out of here myself."

"Okay, then," Thompson said. "We'll wrap this game up tomorrow, one way or another."

"Done," Clint said. "Good night, Ben."

"Night."

Clint entered his room and turned on the lamp. His bed was empty, which was something he regarded as a mixed blessing at best.

He wondered which room Paula was in this morning.

THIRTY-FOUR

When Clint came down to breakfast the next morning, he was once again greeted by the sight of Harry Bartock sitting alone, eating.

"This is getting to be a habit," Bartock said. "Good morning."

"Morning," Clint said. He walked to the kitchen door, stuck his head in, and told the cook he was ready for breakfast.

"Coming right out," she promised, drying her hands on her apron.

Clint went to the table and sat down, leaving the seat between him and Bartock empty.

"So what do you think?" Bartock asked.

"About what?"

"About the game," Bartock said. "You and Ben must have talked about it last night. You think today will be the last day?"

"Do you?"

"Oh yes," Bartock said. "You and Ben should do away with Mr. Griffith, Mr. Mason, and Miss Harrison before the day is out."

"You think so?"

"Oh, yes," Bartock said. "You are obviously the superior poker players."

"Well . . . thank you," Clint said. "And what about you?"

"Oh, I've thoroughly enjoyed myself," Bartock said. "Of course, I would have liked to have had more quality poker players, but it has been a pleasure watching you and Ben play. By the way . . . how much have you won so far?"

Clint looked at Bartock and said, "I wonder if Cook will bring any flapjacks out this morning."

Before long the others came down for breakfast. Clint watched Paula, but if she had found someone else's bed to warm, she wasn't giving it away.

After breakfast they went into the other room and found Jenkins sitting at the table with a sealed deck of cards.

"Not hungry this morning, Jenkins?" Ben Thompson asked.

Jenkins looked at Thompson and said, "I was up very early this morning. I have had my breakfast."

"Well, in that case," Thompson said, seating himself, "let's play poker."

As expected, Jim Griffith ran out of chips after two hands.

"Thanks for nothing," he grumbled, getting up. "I know my way out."

"Thank you, Mr. Griffith," Bartock chirped.

By midday Cort Mason had also tapped out.

"That's it for me, folks," he said, standing up. "It's been a pleasure."

"Thank you for the game, Mr. Mason," Bartock said, shaking the man's hand.

Mason nodded to the others and walked out of the room.

"Well," Bartock said, looking around the table, "we're down to four."

"Looks like it," Thompson said.

"What are we playing?" Bartock asked.

Clint looked at Jenkins and said, "Five-card stud."

"Cards coming out . . ." Jenkins dealt.

Whether or not Paula Harrison had found a man to replace Clint soon became a moot point. Several hours after Mason left, she stood up and looked around the table.

"I'm all done," she said. "Thank you all. It was . . . an education."

She looked at Ben Thompson, who smiled and gave her a little wave. She passed over Clint pointedly and looked at her host.

"Thank you for your hospitality, Harry," she said.

"I'll extend it further, Paula," he said. "There's no hurry for you to leave."

"Thank you," she said. "I think I'll have a bath."

She nodded to the table and walked out.

Clint stared at Bartock, who boldly stared back at him with a smile.

Paula had not only found herself another man, she had latched onto their wealthy host. Well, good for her . . .

"Shall we continue?" Bartock asked. "Just the three of us?"

Thompson looked at Clint, who shrugged and said, "Why not? For a while anyway."

It soon became quite apparent that Clint and Thompson were virtually playing head-to-head. Bartock was simply filling a seat, almost the way Jenkins was. He was no factor in the game at all and for a couple of hours did not take one hand.

Meanwhile, as was the case in most head-to-head endeavors unless both players went all in, Clint and Thompson were playing even.

"This seems silly," Thompson said.

"Yes, it does," Clint said. "We've played virtually even up for the past hour." He looked at Bartock and added, "And you haven't taken a hand. I think it's time to call it quits."

"I have a suggestion," Bartock said.

"What?" Thompson asked.

"Why don't you and Clint go all in and play one last hand?"

Thompson and Clint exchanged glances. They each had a lot of money in front of them.

"That's crazy," Clint said.

"I agree."

Bartock frowned and said, "But I thought that was the way it's done."

"In a winner-takes-all game, yes," Clint said,

"but nothing was said beforehand about this being that kind of game."

"So . . . you won't do that?" Bartock asked, looking disappointed.

"No," Clint said.

"No," Thompson said. "We'll just each take our winnings and leave." He stood up and said, "The game is over. . . ." Then he looked at his host and said, "If that's all right with you?"

"Well, yes, of course," Bartock said. He looked at Jenkins and said, "The game is over, Jenkins."

"Yes, sir."

"Will you gentlemen be staying the night?" Bartock asked.

"I believe I will," Clint said. "Ben?"

"Why not?" Thompson said.

"Excellent," Bartock said. "Dinner will be served in one hour. I will see you gentlemen there."

Bartock got up and left the room, followed closely by Jenkins.

"What do you think of Paula?" Thompson said.

"I guess she figured if she was going to lose the game," Clint said, "why not win the host?"

"He's got a lot of money," Thompson said.

"He does that."

"Leavin' early tomorrow?" Thompson asked.

"I expect so."

"Headin' where?"

"Texas."

Thompson made a face and said, "I think I'll go to San Francisco, find another game." He passed his hand over his forehead and said, "Right now a bath sounds real good to me."

"I think I'll go for a walk," Clint said. "See you at dinner."

"Right."

They left the room and went their separate ways in the foyer.

Outside, in the shadows, Clint counted his money. He had cleared close to twelve thousand dollars, and he was willing to bet that half of it had been lost by Bartock himself.

THIRTY-FIVE

The company at dinner consisted of Bartock, Paula, Ben Thompson, and Clint Adams. The others had already left the ranch.

Bartock and Paula were now making it fairly obvious that they were sleeping together. Most of the conversation was being carried by Bartock, but while he was talking to Clint and Thompson, he was looking at Paula. In return, Paula only had eyes for him.

"Well," Bartock said when dinner was over, "I think it's time for me to turn in. Paula?"

"Yes, Harry," Paula Harrison said dutifully, "me, too."

"Gentlemen," Bartock said, "you'll be leaving in the morning?"

Clint looked at Thompson and then back at Bartock. He, in turn, was looking at Paula Harrison like she was four aces in the hand.

"Yep," Clint said, "we're leaving tomorrow."

"Early," Ben Thompson chimed in, giving Clint the eye.

154   **J. R. ROBERTS**

"Oh yeah," Clint said, nodding his head vigorously, "early."

"Good," Harry Bartock said, standing up and pulling Paula's chair out for her. "It was a very great pleasure playing with you gentlemen and having you as guests in my house."

"Thank—" Thompson started, but Bartock was not listening to him.

"I might not be awake when you leave, though," Bartock said, walking to the door with his arm around Paula's waist. Over his shoulder, he added, "Perhaps we will have a chance to do this again next year?"

"I doubt—" Thompson said, but Bartock and Paula were already gone. Thompson looked at Clint and said, "I doubt it."

"Me, too," Clint said.

Clint was awakened during the night by a light but insistent knocking on his door. He padded barefoot to the door, clad only in his underwear.

It was Paula Harrison. She had a blanket wrapped around her, and she opened her arms, spreading the blanket wide, to show him that she was naked underneath. He looked at her full breasts with their erect nipples and couldn't help but react with desire. He remembered very well what they felt like in his hands and what they had tasted like.

"You have only yourself to blame for this, you know," she said.

At first he had thought that she'd come to him because the game was over, but obviously her intent was to gloat over him. Maybe it was because he had won at the game and she had lost. Perhaps it was just that her ego was still bruised by his refusal of her.

"Isn't Bartock going to miss you?" he asked.

"He's fast asleep," she said. She closed the blanket tightly around her. "I just wanted you to see what you were missing."

"Believe me, Paula," he said, "believe me, I remember."

She stared at him for a few moments. He thought she might be waiting for him to ask her into his room. As attractive as the prospect was, he resisted. He was leaving tomorrow morning, and he didn't need any added complications before then.

"Well . . ." she said. "Maybe we'll meet at another time, in another game."

"I hope so," he said.

She turned, started back down the hall, then turned to face him again.

"Next time," she said, smiling, "I'll beat you."

He wasn't quite sure if she meant at cards, or what?

In the morning Clint and Thompson met at the barn and saddled their own horses. They had not arranged a time to meet, but obviously they were both anxious to get away from Harry Bartock's ranch.

"Not much of a game," Thompson said.

"I was thinking the same thing," Clint said.

"Profitable, though."

Clint leaned his elbow on his saddle and looked at Ben Thompson.

"Yeah, it was profitable, but it wasn't that much fun, you know?"

Thompson nodded and said, "I know."

They mounted up and rode outside. Thompson looked at the house and shook his head.

"What?" Clint asked.

"I'm just wondering how much Paula is going to take Bartock for."

"Was that her plan all along?" Clint asked. "To come here and charm Bartock?"

Thompson looked at Clint and said, "Her plan was to come here and make money. She won't leave until she does, one way or another."

"If that's the case," Clint said, "my guess is that *she's* going to come out of this the big winner."

Thompson looked at Clint and said, "I guess we know who that makes the big loser, right?"

"I only hope he stays a good loser."

Clint and Ben Thompson separated just outside of Gambler's Fork.

"I'm heading for California," Thompson said. "I'll find a game there, maybe San Francisco."

"Try Sacramento," Clint said. "It's an interesting city."

"I'll think about it," Thompson said. "You stayin' here awhile?"

"A couple of days, maybe," Clint said. "There's a lady in town who's worth at least that."

Thompson stuck out his hand, and Clint took it.

"Good luck," Clint said.

"You, too."

Thompson veered off and rode west. Clint watched for a while, then headed for the town of Gambler's Fork—and the good cooking at Red's.

THIRTY-SIX

Clint checked into the hotel and walked over to Red's to see Janet Munro. When he walked in, she was in the act of serving a couple of diners. She straightened, saw him and smiled, and walked over to him.

"How did you do?" she asked.

"I did all right."

"Is it over?"

"Yes."

"Will you be in town for a while?"

"A couple more days."

"Should we waste them?" she asked.

"No," he said with a definite shake of his head, "we should not waste them."

"What?" Harry Bartock cried, sitting straight up in bed. In doing so he caused the sheet to be yanked off of Paula Harrison, giving Jenkins a good look at her naked breasts.

"Harry—" Paula said, reaching for the sheet.

"Shut up!" he said.

Jenkins, who had knocked and entered when told to, remained stoic in the doorway.

"Jenkins, say that again," Bartock said.

Jenkins took a deep breath and said, "It appears that the snaphaunce is gone."

"The *snap*haunce?"

"Yes, sir."

"Stolen?"

"Apparently."

"What do you mean, *apparently*?" Bartock demanded. "It was either stolen or it wasn't."

"Well," Jenkins said, "it's gone, and if you don't have it—"

"Of course I don't!"

"Then it was stolen."

Bartock turned his head and glared at Paula Harrison.

"Well, I didn't take it," she said, shrinking back from him. "I don't even know what it is."

Bartock looked at Jenkins.

"One of the players took it," Bartock concluded.

"It would appear so, sir."

"Get the men," Bartock said. "Go to town and bring somebody back."

"Somebody?"

"Any of the players you find."

"Yes, sir."

"Jenkins!" Bartock called before his man could leave the room.

"Yes, sir?"

"Find Adams, if you can," Bartock said. "Bring me Clint Adams!"

"Yes, sir."

As Jenkins left the room, Bartock stood up and started to dress.

"Get dressed!" he barked at Paula.

"Harry, I don't know what's going—"

"Get dressed, damn it!" Bartock said. "Do as I say!"

Suddenly, he wasn't the man she thought she could lead around by his penis anymore, the man she thought she would be able to take for a lot of money before finally moving on.

Suddenly, he was a dangerous man—a role she had never *imagined* would fit Harry Bartock.

After a few hours Clint Adams decided that Janet Munro was as good in bed as she was in the kitchen.

She was lying next to him, her head cushioned by her forearm and elbow, staring at him.

"I didn't think you'd come back," she said.

"Didn't you?"

"Well," she said, making circles on his belly with her palm, "I *hoped* you'd come back, but I didn't *expect* it."

"You would want a man to do what you expect, would you?" he asked. "Wouldn't that be boring?"

"Not always," she said. "Sometimes it's nice to meet a man who's predictable . . . but not this time."

She leaned over and replaced her palm with her mouth. She kissed his belly, licked him, then dipped her head lower. She peppered his thighs with light kisses, and when she finally took him into her mouth, he moaned and lifted his hips. . . .

"All right," he said, still later, "I have to ask."

"Ask what?"

"Why do they call you Red?"

"Oh," she said, "that's easy. When I was small, I had red hair."

"How could that be?" he asked. "How could you have had red hair when you were small and then blond when you grew up?"

"I don't know," she said. "Well, I'm talking about when I was *really* small—like when I was born. My parents named me Janet, but they always called me Red. When my hair color changed, the name stayed. When I opened the restaurant, I couldn't think of anything else to call it."

He stared at her for a moment, trying to decide whether or not she was telling the truth, and finally decided that she was.

"I believe you."

"Good," she said, sliding her arm over his chest. She was lying on her belly next to him while he was lying on his back. "Then we've established a bond of truth between us."

"I guess we have."

He put his hand on her back and was about to move it down to her butt when suddenly the door was kicked open and the room was filled with men with guns.

THIRTY-SEVEN

Because Janet was lying with her arm over him, his initial move for his gun was impeded just enough for them to get the drop on him.

"Don't," Jenkins said, pointing a shotgun at him. There were four other men with him. They all pointed guns at Clint.

"You sure you got enough men for this, Jenkins?" Clint asked.

Janet was smart enough not to move. She couldn't see the other men, but she kept her eyes on Clint.

"Just playing it safe, Mr. Adams," Jenkins said. "After all, you *do* have a reputation."

"So tell me," Clint said, "is Mr. Bartock a sore loser after all? Is this how he gets his losses back?"

"This is how he gets back what was stolen from him," Jenkins said.

Clint frowned.

"And what was stolen?"

"You don't know?"

"No," Clint said, "I don't."

"Well," Jenkins said, "I won't spoil it. I'll let him tell you, and then you can try to convince him that you didn't take it. Come on, get dressed."

"I want the lady to get dressed in private," Clint said. "That means you and your men will wait out in the hall."

Jenkins regarded Clint over the twin barrels of his shotgun and shook his head.

"The lady does not have to get dressed," Jenkins said. "Just you. She can remain covered on the bed."

"Clint—" Janet said.

"Just lie still," he told her. "Everything will be all right."

He stood up, and the other six people in the room watched him dress. Clint looked at his gun belt hanging off a chair.

"No," Jenkins said, "no gun."

"Then you bring it," Clint said. "I'm not leaving it. I'll want it after I've convinced your boss I didn't take anything."

"Move away," Jenkins said.

Clint complied, and Jenkins instructed one of the other men to get the gun belt and hand it to him. When he had it, he draped it over one shoulder while holding the shotgun with the other hand.

"All right," he said then, "let's go. Please do not try to escape."

"I wouldn't think of it," Clint said, moving toward the door. "I want to find out what this is all about."

At the door Clint turned and looked at Janet, who was sitting up with the sheet held in front of her.

"Don't do anything," he said. "I'll be back."

"The sheriff—"

"No," Clint said, "don't do *anything*. Understand?"

Slowly, she nodded.

Out in the hall Jenkins said, "That was good."

"We don't need the law involved in this, Jenkins," Clint said. "We can settle it among ourselves, don't you think?"

"That," Jenkins said, "will be up to Mr. Bartock."

When they got outside, Clint saw that both Jim Griffith and Tim Easter were being held by half a dozen more men. They were sitting in a buggy, their hands tied behind them, and they had been relieved of their guns.

"You fellas still around?" Clint said.

"What the hell is goin' on here, Adams?" Griffith demanded.

"I don't know."

Easter had a bruise over his eye, and he had only one boot on.

"I knew I shoulda left town right away," he moaned, shaking his head.

"It wouldn't have mattered. We would have tracked you down anyway," Jenkins said.

"What about the others?" Griffith asked. "Mason and Ben Thompson? And the woman? Why should we be the only ones who are—"

"They will be found also," Jenkins said. "Meanwhile, we will all go back to the ranch so that Mr. Bartock can talk to you."

He looked at Clint and said, "Will you join them in the buggy?"

"Don't you want to tie my hands?" Clint asked, holding his hands out.

"That won't be necessary," Jenkins said with a shake of his head. "Please."

Clint obliged and climbed into the buggy. He sat opposite the other two.

"What's goin' on?" Griffith hissed. "Is Bartock welching?"

"Apparently something was stolen from the house," Clint told him.

"What?"

"I don't know. I guess we'll find out when we get there."

THIRTY-EIGHT

When they reached the ranch, Clint stepped down from the buggy and helped each of the bound men down. After warning them not to try anything, Jenkins had them cut loose.

"There's at least a dozen men with guns around us," Griffith said irritably. "What could we try?"

"As for you, Mr. Griffith," Jenkins said, "I would advise you to hold a civil tongue in your head."

"Why, you—"

"He's right," Clint said to Griffith. "Losing your head is not going to do us any good here."

"He's right, Jim," Easter said.

"Okay, okay," Griffith said. He visibly took hold of himself and said in a different tone, "Okay, let's get this over with."

"Inside, gentlemen," Jenkins said. "Mr. Bartock is waiting."

And he was; he was waiting right in the entry hall, hands on hips, Paula Harrison standing beside him. She looked at Clint with pleading eyes when they entered, and he could see that she was frightened. Bartock had a look on his face that Clint had never seen and would never have imagined the man capable of.

He looked *deadly*.

The armed men fanned out and literally surrounded them, so that Clint, Griffith, Easter, Bartock, and Paula were completely encircled.

"What's this all about, Bartock?" Clint demanded.

Bartock opened his mouth as if to speak, then closed it and thought a moment.

"Jenkins," he said when he did speak.

"Sir?"

"Bring Adams."

Bartock turned and walked away, the circle opening to allow him through.

"Follow him," Jenkins said to Clint.

"Hey—" Griffith started, but looks from Clint and Easter silenced him.

Clint followed Harry Bartock down the hall and into his study, all the while aware of Jenkins's shotgun trained on his back.

"Close the door, Jenkins," Bartock said.

Jenkins did so and then stood in front of it, holding the shotgun across his arms.

Bartock went around behind the desk and sat down.

"For what it's worth," he said to Clint, "I don't think *you* took it."

"Took what?"

Bartock studied Clint for a long moment, then said, "The snaphaunce."

"It's missing?" Clint said stupidly. Of course it was. Bartock had just said so.

"It's been *stolen*," Bartock said, "and it had to be one of the players who took it."

"And why not me?"

"You have too much respect for guns," Bartock said. "Besides, you won too much money."

"Then you think one of the losers took it?"

"Yes."

"And you still have your men out looking for Ben Thompson? He was the other winner."

Bartock waved a hand and said, "When they get here with him, I'll let him go."

"And what do you intend to do with the others?"

"Find out who took the snaphaunce."

"And then?"

"Get it back."

"And?"

Bartock hesitated, then said, "I'll decide that when I find out who took the piece and I get it back."

"And if it turns out to be Paula?"

"She would be foolish to take it and remain in the house," Bartock said.

"Or smart enough to do *just that*."

Bartock regarded Clint silently for a few moments—yet again—and then touched his jaw and said, "Yes, yes, I see your point. . . ."

"It's just another option, Harry," Clint said.

"All right then," Bartock said, smiling suddenly, "you will find out who took it."

"Me?"

"That's right," Bartock said. "You talk to Paula, and Griffith and Easter. Find out if they took it. If they didn't, then we know that Cort Mason did."

"And then what?"

"And then you will go and find him."

"And if I refuse?"

Bartock looked past Clint, and suddenly the barrels of the shotgun were in his back.

"That would not be a wise decision," Bartock said.

"No," Clint said, "I guess not."

"Do you agree then?"

"Do I have a choice?"

"No," Bartock said. "You will be my detective."

THIRTY-NINE

Bartock told Clint to use his study, and he would have Jenkins bring each person in one at a time.

Paula was first.

"He's crazy, Clint," she said as she entered.

"Maybe," Clint said, "but something of his has been stolen, and if we don't find it, he might hold us *all* responsible."

"But I—"

"Sit down," Clint said. He was already seated behind Bartock's desk.

She sat across from him.

"Did you take it, Paula?"

"Take what?"

"The snaphaunce."

Either the puzzled look on her face was genuine, or she was a wonderful actress.

"I don't even know what a snap—snap—snap*what* is!" she said.

He studied her a moment longer, and then said, "I believe you."

"Why do *you* have to believe me?" she asked. "Doesn't *he* have to believe me?"

"He's asked me to find out who took the gun."

"It's a gun? Why doesn't he think you took it?"

"Because it *is* a gun, and he thinks I have too much respect for guns to have stolen it."

"Did you steal it?"

"No."

"And now you know I didn't," she said. "That leaves the others."

"Not Ben."

"Why not Ben?"

"The same reason as me."

"So Griffith, Easter, and Mason?"

"Yes."

"Which one do you think took it?"

"I don't know," Clint said. "I can't imagine Mason taking it."

"Why not?"

"He's a gambler," Clint said, "not a thief. He knows he's going to win some and lose some. He wouldn't steal something from Bartock just because he lost at poker."

"Okay," she said, "so that leaves the other two."

He thought a moment, then said, "Not Easter."

"Why not?"

"He's not smart enough, or brave enough, *or* stupid enough for it."

"So that leaves Griffith."

"Yes," Clint said thoughtfully, "he'd do it, if he thought he could get away with it, but . . ."

"But what?"

"He wouldn't stay around town if he took it."

"Maybe he would to make it *look* like he didn't take it," she suggested.

It was basically the same thing he had said to Bartock about her.

"Griffith is smart," Clint said, "but I don't know if he's that devious."

"So what are you saying?"

"I'll talk to Griffith next," he said. "I'll know something after that. Have Jenkins send him in next, Paula."

"All right," she said. She stood up and walked to the door, but turned before she opened it.

"Clint?"

"What?"

"You have to get me out of here," she said. "You have to take me with you when you leave."

"Don't worry, Paula," he promised, "I will."

FORTY

When Griffith entered the room, he closed the door solidly behind him and then started to look around.

"Is there another way out?" he asked. "Can we get out that window?"

"We're not going anywhere, Griffith," Clint said. "They'd just run us down before we could get very far. Sit down."

"You look comfortable," Griffith said, grudgingly taking a seat. "What's going on?"

"We have to see this through to the end."

"And what *is* the end?"

"Getting Bartock's . . . property back."

"What property? What was taken?"

"You don't know?"

"No," Griffith said, "I don't know. Who said I did?"

"Nobody."

Griffith remained silent for a few moments, then apparently out of curiosity said, "What was taken?"

173

"A gun."

"A *gun*? Why would I take a gun? I *have* guns."

"A very valuable gun," Clint said.

"I didn't see any valuable guns around."

"Bartock has a collection, well hidden. One of them is missing, and he thinks that one of us took it."

"So why are you sitting behind his desk?"

"He satisfied himself that I didn't take it," Clint said. "Now he wants me to find out who did."

"And you want to pin it on me?"

"I want to find out who took it, Griffith," Clint said, "so the rest of us can get out of here."

"Well, I didn't take it," Griffith said. "Where was the damn thing anyway?"

"It was in the room where we were playing."

"Well," Griffith said, "that settles it. That room was guarded like a fortress. None of us could have got in there to steal it."

Griffith had a point. Bartock did have the room well guarded, which brought up an interesting possibility.

"All right," Clint said.

"All right what?"

"Tell Bartock to come in."

"But . . . you ain't talked to Easter yet. Don't you want to talk to Tim?"

"You think he took it?"

"He wouldn't have the nerve," Griffith said. Now the man sat forward and added, "Just between you and me, I *wanted* to rob the place, but I couldn't get him to go along with it."

"Why not do it alone?"

Griffith sat back.

"Ain't my style."

No, Clint thought, it wouldn't be. He'd have to have someone to throw to the wolves if things got rough. In fact, if he *had* taken the snaphaunce, he probably *would* have tried to blame Easter. . . .

"Okay," Clint said, "send in Bartock."

"What are you gonna tell him?" Griffith asked. "That I took it?"

"You didn't take it, Griffith," Clint said. "I know that."

"Then who did?"

"I think I know."

"Who?" Griffith asked. "Tell me."

"Never mind." Clint shook his head and waved at the man to leave the room. "Just tell Bartock to come back in."

Griffith reluctantly left the room, and Clint went through Bartock's drawers, found what he wanted, and then settled back in Bartock's chair to wait.

FORTY-ONE

When Harry Bartock came back into the room, he was followed by Jenkins. That suited Clint just fine.

"You didn't talk to all of them yet," Bartock said. "What's going on?"

"I don't have to talk to all of them," Clint said. "I know who took the piece."

"You do?" Bartock asked. "Already?"

"Yes."

"All right then," Bartock said. "Who took it?"

Clint sat back in his chair and regarded the two men silently.

"One of you," he finally said.

"What?" Bartock said.

"Preposterous," Jenkins said, eyeing Clint closely. He was still holding the shotgun crossways, but it wouldn't have taken much for him to straighten it out and point it.

"You can't be serious," Bartock said.

"Who else would be able to get into that

room past the security, Harry? Only you or Jenkins."

"Yes, but . . . I didn't take it," Bartock said. He turned then and looked at Jenkins.

"You don't believe him, do you?" Jenkins demanded.

"He's right about one thing, Jenkins," Bartock said. "Only you or I could have gotten past those guards . . . and I know *I* didn't do it."

"That leaves you, Jenkins," Clint said. "You stole the piece. Harry, I think you'll find the snaphaunce in Jenkins's room."

"Jenkins—" Bartock started, but Jenkins swung the shotgun around and clipped his "boss" across the jaw with it.

Bartock went flying across the room.

"Damn you!" Jenkins snarled and brought the rifle around to bear on Clint.

Clint stood up quickly and pointed the gun he had found in Bartock's desk drawer. He pulled the trigger and then dove away from the desk as the shotgun went off. Both barrels erupted, blowing out the window behind the desk.

Clint rolled, slammed painfully into a wall, and looked at Jenkins, ready to fire Bartock's .32 Colt again, but there was no need.

Jenkins stood with his back flat against the door. There was a red stain spreading on his chest, and as he started to slide to the floor, a trickle of blood ran from his mouth. The shotgun hit the floor a moment before he did.

Clint went to Bartock and helped him up. He

had a welt on his jaw, but he didn't seem to be seriously hurt.

"That was fantastic!" he said. "Where did you get the gun?"

"I figured a gun lover like you would have one in your desk," Clint said.

"Yes," Bartock said, "I'd forgotten. You—you killed him before he could kill you with the shotgun. It was incredible."

Outside the door someone was shouting and banging on it. Clint ignored the commotion, walked to Jenkins, and checked to make sure he was dead.

"How long did he work for you?" Clint asked.

"Years!" Bartock said.

Clint stood up and faced Bartock.

"Maybe you should have treated him better."

"I paid him," Bartock said. "He betrayed me."

"You paid him, sure," Clint said, "but like I said, maybe you should have treated him better. I guess he finally got fed up and saw a chance to make off with something of value, knowing you'd blame someone else."

"Well," Bartock said, "he didn't count on meeting up with the Gunsmith, did he?"

Clint stared at Harry Bartock, feeling intense distaste for the man. He roughly handed Bartock his .32, then walked to the body and moved it away from the door.

Outside the foyer was filled. He spotted Paula.

"What happened, Clint?" she asked.

He looked at her and asked, "You still want to leave?"

"Well—yes, of course."

"Then let's go," he said, taking her arm. "We're leaving . . . now!"

If you enjoyed this book, subscribe now and get...

TWO FREE

A $7.00 VALUE–

A special offer for people who enjoy reading the best Westerns published today.

WESTERNS!

NO OBLIGATION

Mail the coupon below

To start your subscription and receive 2 FREE WESTERNS, fill out the coupon below and mail it today. We'll send your first shipment which includes 2 FREE BOOKS as soon as we receive it.